Maniac Drifter

Essential Prose Series 125

Maniac Drifter

Laura Marello

GUERNICA
EDITIONS
TORONTO • BUFFALO • LANCASTER (U.K.)
2016

Michael Mirolla, editor
Cover design and interior layout: David Moratto
Guernica Editions Inc.
1569 Heritage Way, Oakville, (ON), Canada L6M 2Z7
2250 Military Road, Tonawanda, N.Y. 14150-6000 U.S.A.
www.guernicaeditions.com

Distributors:
University of Toronto Press Distribution,
5201 Dufferin Street, Toronto (ON), Canada M3H 5T8
Gazelle Book Services, White Cross Mills, High Town,
Lancaster LA1 4XS U.K.

First edition.
Printed in Canada.

Legal Deposit—Third Quarter
Library of Congress Catalog Card Number: 2016938890
Library and Archives Canada Cataloguing in Publication
Marello, Laura, author
Maniac drifter / Laura Marello. -- First edition.

(Essential prose series ; 125)
Issued in print and electronic formats.
ISBN 978-1-77183-065-2 (paperback).--ISBN 978-1-77183-066-9 (epub).
--ISBN 978-1-77183-067-6 (mobi)

I. Title. II. Series: Essential prose series ; 125

PS3613.A7397M36 2016 813'.6 C2016-902166-1 C2016-902167-X

for my mother

Provincetown,
Cape Cod,
Summer 1985

Chapter One

Friday

I woke up Friday morning in bed with a man I didn't know. Of course I had seen him around town. His name was Getz. He was thin and muscular, had fine features and a sexy, angular face that promised mystery. When I had asked about him, everyone in town had warned me that Getz was a coke dealer. Almost everyone who had been in Provincetown for more than ten years had dealt drugs at one time or another. They were just mad at Getz because the Zanzibar had been the best hangout in town in the seventies; he had been the manager and bartender. They blamed him for it closing down. They said he skimmed money, embezzled it, lost it, mismanaged everything. Now he was a lobsterman.

But a lot of people had done that. The scenario went like this: a guy came to town, dealt dope until he had enough money to start a restaurant, made a lot of money at the restaurant, but got greedy and kept dealing. Then he began to throw his weight around in town politics, leaning on people, making them mad. That was usually when the Feds came in, shut his place down until he paid his taxes, or indicted him on a drug traffic charge. Provincetown was like an ongoing B-movie; the restaurant owners, bar owners and bartenders were the movie stars. One star got indicted about every five years or so, always through a similar chain of events. This raised him from star status to Town Hero.

I'm in a movie, I thought as I sat up in bed. *This town's a goddamn movie.* That's when I looked around the room and realized I wasn't at home.

I walked out onto the porch and saw that a flying buttress in the shape of a voluptuous woman was nailed above the door lintel. I knew right away that I was at the Figurehead House. I could see the bay on the other side of Commercial Street, the gutted Ice House down the hill on the water side. It was sunny, and a slight breeze blew off the water. No one was awake yet; the tourists had not come in from up-Cape. I walked down the hill toward home.

I lived on the top floor of a white house on Bradford Street that had been converted into apartments. It would have been impertinent to lock the door. A black leather jacket and felt fedora were hanging on the crank handle to the skylight. Harper Martin, the owner of these sartorial gems, was asleep on the day bed in the kitchen. I had never woken up in the morning and found myself in bed with Harper Martin. I wondered if it would be different with him, if I would be able to remember.

Harper always played the part of the friendly sleuth, with his jacket and fedora, his jaunty walk and manner. But was he really a sleuth or just acting one? I could never determine. He drove a silver Corvette that said *Maniac Drifter* on the bumper, and had wooed his last girlfriend by singing her rock songs across the parking lot of Days Studios, where they were both painters-in-residence. He wrote the tunes himself. "Is-a-bel-la! The stock market crumbles when I speak your name!" was the chorus to one.

The skylight was cranked all the way open; I stuck my head out and looked at the bay. I had a view of the water between the Ice House and the neighboring roof. A few lobster boats and trawlers headed toward the breakwater. The gulls whizzed past my head. This apartment was in the gull zone, intruding on their airspace. They liked to dive-bomb anyone who stood under the skylight, and then pull out at the last minute.

"Hey," Harper said. The noise of the gulls must have woken him up.

"French toast?"

Harper climbed out of the day bed and slipped his chinos on, then his white shirt and string tie, then he sat on the bed and put on his black socks and wing tips.

I grilled the French toast while he set the table, humming as he walked around the kitchen. Suddenly, as he was folding a napkin, he belted out: "Romance without finance is a nuisance (you ain't kiddin' brother!). Mama, Mama, please give up that gold." He came up behind me at the stove and looked over my shoulder. "Wanna come to El Salvador with me and break up marriages? You can chase after the husband; I'll go for the wife."

For a moment I thought he knew about my trouble and was making light of it, but he couldn't know. I hadn't told him, and it wasn't simple enough to guess.

"See what I care," he said. "Wanna be the lead singer in my New Wave band?"

"Bring me the plates," I said. He brought them. I slid the French toast on to them. I asked him why he smelled like a lobsterman.

"I was sitting next to one last night," he said. "The lobsterman's name was Getz."

"How do you know he is a lobsterman?"

He poured a dollop of syrup on his French toast. "Hey, babe, I may be from Los Angeles, but after two years in this joint I can tell the Yankees, Portuguese, lobstermen, artists, hippies and gays apart."

When we had finished eating, Harper took the empty plates to the sink and ran water over them. He bellowed: "You're so good and you're so fine, you ain't got no money you can't be mine, it ain't no joke to be stone broke, Baby, Baby, I'm not lying when I say that—"

"Why'd you spend the night on the day bed?"

"I'm running from the law." He put on his jacket and fedora, tipped his hat, bowed graciously, and shut himself in the bathroom. I licked the rim of the syrup bottle. I could hear the shower running and Harper singing, "You must remember this, a kiss is just a kiss, a sigh is just a sigh. The fundamental things apply as time goes by."

Harper was right about his categories: Yankees, Portuguese, fishermen, artists, hippies and gays—that was Provincetown. The Pilgrims landed first, and settled out on Long Point, a spit of sand that curled to a tip out past the edge of town. You would have to walk through marshes or over a breakwater to get to it now. It was too cold and windy for them there, so eventually they went to Plymouth. But people kept coming and settled out on Long Point, to fish mainly, and eventually some moved into town. When no one lived out on the Point anymore, they brought the houses into town and affixed blue historical plaques to them.

After the Yankees, the Portuguese came over, also to fish, and they had been here ever since. Now they lived on the northwest side of town, behind all the tourist traffic on Bradford Street, just beyond Shankpainter Pond, in modest houses where no one would bother them.

The artists first came in the 1880s; Charles Hawthorne was the most famous of the group. They came again in the 1920s, among them were Edwin Dickinson, Eugene O'Neill and the Provincetown Players. Dickinson lived in Days Studios; the Art Association and Beachcombers were formed. In the thirties and forties the Abstract Expressionists came from New York; Motherwell and Frankenthaler used the barn at Days Studios. Cosmo and his group of Rhode Island painters joined the Art Association and Beachcombers. Galleries sprung up, each with its allegiances and rivalries. Now, in the eighties, Cosmo and his circle remained in town, while most of the Abstract Expressionists summered in the Hamptons, except for Motherwell, who had stayed in Provincetown and moved his studio from Days into his home on the East End. Days Studios was now used by the young up-and-coming painters like Harper Martin, most of whom came in from New York for winter residencies. Some stayed on when summer came.

The hippies came over in the sixties and they were the attraction for that time, Provincetown being prone to fads, being Mecca for whatever fad came. But some of them stayed and now they did things around town that suited them. Angelo Fontana was a whale and seal expert. Other hippies that had stayed worked as leathersmiths or bartenders, one had become an orchid specialist and park ranger, some of them learned how to fish, some dealt drugs or worked for the nonprofit radio station.

The gays had been in town since the 1950s, but did not become really visible until the last ten years when their lifestyle became fashionable. Since Provincetown was the end of the road, with nothing beyond it, no one could come through on their way somewhere else. They could only come because they chose to. So the gays figured if people did not like their lifestyle, they could leave. And since they were the most disdained newcomers, nobody listened to them. While no one was listening, they made a lot of money. The women bought restaurants, bars and guest houses. They employed their own lawyer and real estate agent. The men owned bars, restaurants, clothing stores, hairstyling salons, gourmet food shops. They also had a real estate agent of their own. The gays controlled most of the nightclub acts in town; there were two main transvestites, Montana Devon and Gerty. The women had this incredible French Canadian singer named Christianne who was a combination Edith Piaf and Judy Garland in a tuxedo. She sang duets with her wife, Paula. And most everyone slept around—the hippies, the painters, the gays. I liked it that way; it made my problem easier to conceal.

Harper reappeared in the kitchen a half hour later, fully dressed, with his jacket and fedora on. He bowed gravely and thanked me for the use of my shower.

"No problem," I said.

"Wanna run away to El Salvador with me?" he asked

again. He had just returned from a trip to Nicaragua. When I had asked him why he went there, he said because it was "the happening thing." I figured he would go to Poland or Lebanon or South Africa next, but El Salvador sounded practical.

"You never told me why you slept on the day bed last night," I said. He would not ask me where I had slept, but it wasn't out of a sense of propriety. It was as if he knew it was a dangerous subject, and should not be broached.

"I told you, I'm a fugitive from the law." He opened the door. "Well I'm off. See you in a few minutes." He bowed, and shut the door behind him.

On the way to the law office I wondered if Harper were just kidding, or really in trouble, wondered if he were acting the part of the sleuth or was really the sleuth, wondered if he were pretending to be in a movie or if he really was the movie. "This town is a movie," I said out loud. "I'm in a goddamn movie."

***

There were two law offices in town, but since I worked at the one which belonged to Ruth Allen Esquire, I called it by its generic name, *the law office*, as if it were the only law office in town, the way I referred to Cosmo's as *the restaurant* and men referred to their wives as *the wife*. Ruth Allen had her offices on the bottom floor of her big white house on Commercial Street on the east end of town, near Getz's Figurehead House.

Ruth was a small, robust woman with curly brown hair and sparkly black eyes. She had a keen intellect and a devilish curiosity, a sharp wit and hot temper. She was always full of energy, sexy and unselfconscious.

I knew the other town businessmen with movie star status would be at the Maniac Drifter investors' meeting: Cosmo, Antaeus, Falzano. But I had not expected Raphael Souza to be there. I did not think Harper would want to approach him, or even know how. People were embarrassed by tragedy. They did not know how to act after it struck, what to say to the survivors. But there he was, Raphael Souza, sitting in Ruth's office with the other movie stars, when I arrived 15 minutes late.

The Souza family was Provincetown's version of the Kennedys. It was one of the most influential families in town. Jack Souza, 50 years old and the younger of the two brothers, was the president of Provincetown National Bank. The older brother, Raphael Souza, had been running a successful fishing fleet in town for 30 years, and was very influential on the wharf. For the past ten years he also owned the most popular gay bar and disco in town, the White Sands. He lived in the old family house, huge and white, on the west end of Commercial Street, with his boyfriend Tommy and his sheepdog Zac. Copies of Roman statues sat on the finely clipped front lawn. A flagpole stood near the gate; at sunrise Tommy raised the American and Portuguese flags on it, at sunset he lowered them. The eight-foot mesh fence that surrounded the property was entwined with honeysuckle vines. Some nights, on my walk home from Cosmo's, I leaned against the fence, stuck my fingers into the honeysuckle, and watched the top of the house, where a blue light shone in the cupola.

Raphael Souza had been divorced despite the fact that

the family was devout Catholic. In those days he sometimes left his fishing fleet to his captains and sailed down the coast to Newport with a pretty girl. When Jack's daughter Julie was little, she had a lot of fun with Raphael and his daughter Annie on the boats, and seemed to prefer Raphael's company to her own father's. This caused bad feeling between the brothers. Their sister Elaine Barry, who was divorced and still lived in town, had tried to bring the brothers back together but nothing worked. A rumor circulated that Raphael was the biggest dope smuggler on Cape Cod Bay. Eventually Jack accused him of using their daughters to transact special deals in Boston, where they attended prep school and then college.

Once Jack had accused Raphael the disasters escalated, as if bringing the danger into the open had unleashed it. First Antaeus' mother killed the Souzas' mother in a hit and run accident. Raphael, being the oldest, inherited the family house. Just after he moved in, his daughter Annie was murdered in Boston by a dope dealer. Annie's mother committed suicide. Raphael took a boyfriend, Tommy, into the house, saying that he would never go near another woman, all his women had been killed—his mother, his daughter, his wife —and that maybe it was his fault, maybe he had a King Midas curse with women, destroying them from greed. Jack never forgave him for bringing Tommy into the family house.

Raphael Souza had already attained movie star status by the time his mother was killed, so when his daughter Annie was murdered he became a Town Hero. With his wife's suicide Raphael was elevated to the highest status possible in Provincetown: Martyr. Raphael even looked like a Christ figure, with his long, curly gray hair and full beard

—only the cigars he and Tommy smoked ruined the image. But the locals didn't care about the martyr status, they were in love with the idea that this family was Provincetown's version of the Kennedys. They were handsome, glamorous, Catholic and doomed. Didn't a suicide, murder and fatal accident compare to assassinations, plane crashes on the Riviera and Chappaquiddick? The glamor of the Souzas was smaller scale certainly, they were not rich and the brothers were not Presidents, but the Provincetown locals liked to imagine that the big white house with the cupola, the pristine lawn with its statues, was like the Kennedy compound at Hyannis Port; and the brave, handsome brothers who were plagued with accidents and tragedies, due in part to their own weaknesses, were simultaneously charmed and hexed the way the Kennedy brothers had been.

"Sorry I'm late," I said when I entered the investors' meeting. Ruth was ensconced behind her desk, talking on the telephone, presiding over the movie stars. She always felt magnanimous toward me at these moments, when large groups of people were watching. She waved her free hand in the air as if to say, *No problem*, and pointed to the empty chair where she meant for me to sit down.

The chairs were arranged in a half-moon shape facing Ruth's desk. It looked like a United Nations meeting, or a panel of experts. Each investor had a black vinyl three-ring binder in his lap. I sat down next to Harper. While Ruth talked into the phone and tapped numbers into her adding machine, Harper bounced one leg up and down, causing his fedora to jump in his lap. Ruth hung up the phone. "Okay," she said, "the bank's confirmed my figures." She rummaged through some papers.

"I won't read through all the Articles of Incorporation because most of them are standard. As you know, the corporation will be called Maniac Drifter Inc., and Harper will act as the officers: president, vice president, secretary and treasurer. The added clause concerns each investor's share, and the privacy of corporate activities. It says: Article VIII Investors agree to grant officers of Maniac Drifter Inc., to wit, Harper Martin, complete privacy as to the nature of the corporation's activities. An Investor may audit the corporate books only when said investor's percentage of return has dropped below the agreed upon rate, or the corporation's treasurer, to wit, Harper Martin, is late by more than thirty days in his monthly return payment. Okay, Kate is going to pass out these envelopes."

Ruth handed them to me.

"The sheet inside states your amount of investment, percentage of return and calculated monthly payment. These will be listed in Appendix A of the Articles. I was just on the phone to Jack at the bank and he verified the figures, so they should be okay."

I passed out the envelopes to the all-star cast there that day, the best and brightest of the movie-star status in Provincetown, all together in one room. It was like ensemble acting. The office was riddled with the widest range of personal, legal and financial disasters imaginable. Of course Cosmo had had an affair with his partner's wife, and Raphael suffered from a female trinity: his daughter was murdered, his mother run over, and his wife had committed suicide. But Antaeus and Falzano also had tragic histories. You could not achieve movie star status in Provincetown without it. Antaeus was known for the events five years before which had raised him temporarily from movie star status to Town Hero. He was indicted on Federal drug traffic charges in the summer, and in the fall his mother killed Raphael Souza's mother in the hit and run auto accident. Then his Bad Attitude Cinema was mysteriously arsoned. Locals referred to that incident as the *Fall Arson Festival*.

Giulia Falzano had her own tragedy. She owned Paradiso's, the women's disco, when Christianne moved down from Montreal looking for a singing job. Falzano hired her to perform Edith Piaf numbers as a second act to Paula, Falzano's wife and business partner. By the third summer Christianne and Paula were singing together. They worked up a routine and went on tour alone that winter. They came home lovers. Falzano had to break up another long-standing relationship, Anna and Jill, to replace Paula. Jill, in turn, disrupted a long-standing relationship to get Esther. Falzano had a sense of humor about it; she called this *Dyke Dominoes*.

My worst fear was an incident like one of these, a careless mistake that caused someone harm or loss, a mistake you couldn't live with, you couldn't face anyone after. How could Antaeus' mother come back to town when she knew she had killed Mrs. Souza? How could Cosmo stay in town when everyone knew he had had an affair with Nello's wife? How could Falzano watch Paula and Christianne sing at the club every night, when Christianne had taken Paula away from her?

This was the way things worked in a small town, in a family, in public life, but I couldn't imagine being in any of those positions. Cedric had always told me I was not tough enough. "Tough as nails!" he said was what I had to be. "Hard as a ball bearing!" But I wasn't. I was a coward. And with my amnesia, I was especially afraid I might cause someone harm.

I finished passing out the envelopes to the investors, and sat down. I looked over at Harper. Now he was taking on his investors' legacy. What disasters would visit him, once he started this Maniac Drifter corporation? What part of the legacy would he inherit? The movie stars were opening their envelopes. "It's like the Oscars," Antaeus said, and in his best Cary Grant voice added: "The envelope please. And the winner is—." Then he started talking to Raphael about the killer whale he had seen in the harbor. Raphael explained that killer whales were really dolphins, and harmless. They did not eat people. Some of the lobstermen had been swimming with it. I thought: Antaeus' mother had killed Raphael's and they were sitting next to each other talking about an Orca in the harbor. These people were too sophisticated to live.

Ruth asked them if the figures were correct. They nodded. "Okay," she said, "the end of Article VIII reads: It is further understood by the investors that however private, all business transactions will comply with the spirit and letter of the law, within the realm of business activities sanctioned by the United States Federal Government and the Commonwealth of Massachusetts."

"Is that necessary?" Cosmo said. "Doesn't it go without saying?"

Ruth looked at Harper. "We decided to add it because of the secrecy clause," she said. "Harper wanted it clear that, not only are the investors uninformed of the activities of the company, they expressly don't sanction, condone or support any illegal activities." Cosmo nodded his head.

"That doesn't absolve us from legal liability," Falzano said.

"That's correct," Ruth said. "Well, the rest is standard. All I need now are your checks."

The investors opened their black vinyl three ring binders. Inside were pages and pages of checks, three per page, with the information stubs off to the left by the metal rings. It was quiet for a moment while everyone wrote. Then the investors began to tear their checks out, fold them in two, and hand them to Ruth. She looked carefully at each one, and compared the figures to hers.

Everyone stood up; each investor shook hands with Harper. It was a rite of passage, the older movie stars acknowledging the talented young movie star on the rise, and welcoming him into their group, like when Bogart made his big break by playing the outlaw in *The Petrified Forest* with Bette Davis and Leslie Howard. Cosmo, Antaeus, Raphael and that group—they were the older generation now. Harper was the new generation.

"The checks will be deposited in your Maniac Drifter account by bank closing this afternoon," Ruth told Harper. He bowed. They shook hands. He tipped his hat.

When I was walking out the door, Ruth yelled: "Wait, wait, come back here." I re-entered the room and waited until everyone left. Ruth shut the door. She pointed out the window, across the street to the Figurehead House. "I told you that Getz was bad news. I told you he's a dealer."

I opened my mouth to speak. Finally I said, "I'm a sucker for a pretty face."

"Have you ever noticed the mural at Animus Pizza?" Ruth said. "Joe Houston painted that. Let me introduce you to him. He's a nice guy. He runs the projectors at the Bad Attitude Cinema. Nice build."

I didn't know what to say, so I just stood there.

"I'm going to introduce you to Joe Houston," Ruth said. "Now will you get out of here?"

***

After work at Cosmo's restaurant that night, I walked home on Commercial Street. A lot of cars were parked at the Beachcombers and the Art Association seemed to be opening a show, because a crowd of well-dressed people was milling around carrying plastic cups of white wine in their hands. I didn't recognize anyone I knew so I kept walking. The sky was clear and the air seemed thin and sharp; it had a bite to it like mountain air at high altitude. It wasn't foggy and languid the way beach air usually was. I walked down the hill past Ruth's house and the Figurehead House, looking at the lights in the different windows.

At the bottom of the hill, at the gutted Ice House, a mangy cat padded out from under the abandoned truck there. While the cat walked in circles around me. I bent down to pet it. I looked up at the truck and the Ice House. On the enormous brick and concrete building with its gaping open spaces, a sign was posted, saying that the Ice House would be converted into condominiums. The sign showed a renovated Ice House with window boxes full of flowers, striped umbrellas on a plank-board patio, and a rebuilt wharf with figures sunbathing on lounge chairs. But the sign had been posted there for a year now and no work had been started. Edward the real estate agent owned the building, but he had not sold enough condos on speculation to fund the renovation.

Locals kept their eye on the truck over the year, figuring it would be the first thing to go if the project ever got underway. But the big green hauler still sat there. All four tires were flat, someone had thrown a brick through the front windshield, a load of torn-up siding with rusty nails was piled in the flat bed. The Ice House itself looked just as bad. If there had ever been windows, they were all gone by now. Some of the large rectangular gaps had been boarded up, but the boards were partially ripped off. The brickwork was crumbling in places, and even the concrete was cracked, and large chunks of it were missing, revealing the steel supports inside.

With the vandalized truck next to it, all the weeds and the battered chain-link fence, the Ice House looked like a bombed out building in a war zone. From the back it looked even more ominous, because the ground floor was open and most of the upper levels were almost completely exposed to the water and offshore wind. The walls had acquired a layer of moss and mold; vines crept up the sides and across the floors.

While I was petting the cat and looking up at the Ice House, wondering if this were what Beirut looked like, I noticed a light shining on one of the interior walls on the fourth floor. It bounced around, disappeared, then reappeared through another opening. At first I thought it might be the beam from one of the lighthouses at Long Point, but then I realized they were too far away to make that small and precise a light on the wall in the Ice House. Anyway, the angle was wrong. Some curious passerby might be shining a light into the place from the ground on the water side, but again, the angle was wrong. The light had to be coming from inside, and on the fourth floor. How did someone get up there, I wondered, and why? The cat rubbed his bony head against my ankle.

I crossed the front of the Ice House, reached the far side I headed toward the back, hugging the wall. I wondered what they were doing up there.

When I reached the end of the building I squinted into the breeze gusting off the water. I could see a boat docked on the wrecked wharf behind the Ice House, Getz's boat. While I was scrutinizing the boat that mangy cat scrambled up to me from behind, as if it had been spooked. It overshot me, with its spiny back arched and its claws out, squealed, and went skidding around the back of the building. The cat's speed sent its back legs off in one direction and its body in the other, like a car spinning out. The cat corrected itself and began to prance forward, until it was out of sight behind the building. "Psst, kitty. Psst, kitty," a voice whispered, as if that were the way to call a cat. It was Getz's voice.

"Hey, what the hell," Harper Martin said from somewhere up above. "I'm up here getting my pants dirty and you're playing with a cat."

"It was crying," Getz said. "Some Tom is probably after it."

I peeked around the corner. Getz was standing on the ground with the cat in his hands. He looked up at Harper, who was on the fourth floor, at the ledge. They both had work gloves on, and a forklift machine was backed halfway inside the building on the ground floor, the lift jacked up to where Harper was standing.

"These cats come with the building," Getz said. "There's probably a half dozen."

"Cats!" Harper said. "Cats! Have they gotten inside the crates? Are there cats at Hatches Harbor?"

Getz put the cat down and shook his head. "Worry about the damp air wrecking your merchandise. Don't worry about the cats."

Harper disappeared behind the wall. Getz lowered the platform on the loaded forklift and backed the machine onto the dock. Then Harper reappeared on the ground. While they were loading the crates onto the boat I realized that, unless Harper got in the boat with Getz, he would be leaving soon, and I was standing at the only exit, since there was a chain link fence around the other side of the building, and the ground floor was sealed shut in front. Harper put his hat on and shook hands with Getz. Getz got in the boat; Harper started in my direction. I scrambled across the dirt lot toward Bradford Street and my apartment.

***

Hatches Harbor was the last stretch of beach at Herring Cove, past the gay beach where there were dunes and biting flies, past the lesbian beach, the family beach (that was near the hot dog stand), past the fishermen. At dawn I parked at the far end of Herring Cove Beach lot, closest to Hatches Harbor. Then, armed with a crowbar, I walked all the way to Race Point, where a sign on the low picket fence said, *TERNS NESTING AREA/ OFF LIMITS*. Angelo, the whale and seal expert, had told me that the terns were an endangered species on the Cape, so when they started nesting at

Hatches Harbor the Forest Service had fenced the area off to prevent tourists from driving them away. I could not see any terns from where I was standing behind the fence. The shore went around the bend there, at a convex angle that obstructed the view. I walked along the fence toward Hatches Harbor Lighthouse. The terns seemed to congregate by the shore, in the low grassy dunes, and left the lighthouse to the seagulls.

Hatches Harbor Light looked rusty and abandoned. The white paint was peeling off around the outer walls and the iron walkway just below the light was missing its railing in places. Thick cords of electrical wire twisted in large cables from a wooden shed to the lighthouse. On the door a sign said: DANGER: HIGH VOLTAGE. DO NOT ENTER. The rusty metal door to the lighthouse stood slightly ajar.

I could hear a humming sound and wondered if it were the high voltage wires. Then I noticed there was a dense brown paste of flying insects in the air, covering the shed and walls of the lighthouse. They started to buzz around my head. They were dragonflies.

The wind was blowing, and no one else around for miles. I stopped in the low grassy dunes. Someone was walking out the lighthouse door. It was Harper. Getz came out behind him. They headed toward the shore, right through the middle of the Terns Nesting Area.

I crouched on the far side of the fence and took a parallel path back to the shore. When I arrived I crept up the shore a few yards, trying to camouflage myself among the low dunes, found a safe vantage point, sat down and watched.

Getz's boat was idling in the water. Harper and Getz were standing on shore near the boat, talking. Angelo was poised on his windsurfer out a little distance beyond the boat, zig-zagging back and forth through the water. I wondered how he got involved in this. In the summer Angelo conducted the whale watch tours on the Dolphin II; throughout the year he spent his free time at the Terns Nesting Area or Race Point, observing the seals. Sometimes he used his windsurfer for transportation.

The Voodoo Woman was walking through the dunes toward Harper and Getz in her leopard outfit. It was a one-piece cream color skin suit with black spots on the legs and torso. Over the leotard she wore a tunic that swept around her in folds, like the draperies on a Greek sculpture. She wore a thick black leather belt around the waist of the tunic, with a silver buckle that had a leopard's face imprinted in it. The leopard was baring its teeth. Usually she wore black canvas elf shoes or for the evening, black leather ankle boots with stiletto heels made out of teak. But today she was barefoot, and had on layers of ankle bracelets that jangled when she walked. When she reached the spot where the three men were standing, she started dancing around them, swooshing her tunic this way and that in the wind. She was chanting an incantation, and shaking the layers of bracelets around her wrists. Getz and Harper climbed into the boat and sailed off. Angelo picked the Voodoo Woman up on the windsurfer, and rode away with her.

When they were out of view, I stood up and walked through the dunes out to the shore, and down to the other side of the fence. I returned to the lighthouse, stepping carefully among the seagulls. I waved the crowbar around my head to keep the dragonflies off. I wondered if they liked the electricity, or the damp, brackish air.

As I approached the lighthouse door, a crowd of seagulls lifted up off the ground and flapped above my head. Some circled the top of the lighthouse, and some were crowded on the steps. I walked up the steps and went inside the lighthouse. The cavernous room was empty except for a half dozen crates that were stacked at the far end, a canvas tarp thrown over the top. I folded back the tarp. The crates were wooden, had no markings, and were hammered together strong and solid.

It took about 20 minutes, but finally I had a lid off. This crate was filled with straw and sawdust. I put my hand in and moved the straw carefully until I could see something. It was a grey, porous stone material. I pushed away more straw, revealing the side of a face, an ear. I uncovered the rest, and pulled it out.

It was a little man made out of pumice or lava. He was sitting cross-legged with his forearms resting on his knees. A plain smooth mask stretched over his face and the top of his head, with holes for the eyes, mouth and ears. The mask was tied with strings at the back of the head, in an elaborate knot carefully etched in the stone.

A plain jumpsuit stretched tight over his arms and legs. There were no markings on it, except for a few stitches over the heart. The jumpsuit was tied with strings in the back at the shoulders, and lower, at the kidneys. Again, the elaborate bow ties were etched carefully in the stone. At the stone man's wrists, limp hands dangled down from his jumpsuit the same size as his own hands. It was as if he had stepped into another man's skin, but for some reason was reluctant to put on the other man's hands.

I set the little skin-suit man down on the crate next to

the open one, and reached back into the straw. I moved it around until I could see a shape, then brushed the straw away from it. The object felt like clay, and was the color of sand. When I had moved enough straw away to recognize its shape, I pulled the figure out. It was a clay woman, with one head but two faces, right next to each other, as if it were a record of a sudden movement, leaving the image of her face in both positions; like a Picasso drawing of multiple profiles. The woman had a long strand of hair over each shoulder that fell down almost to her navel. Her stubby arms reached only part way down her long thin torso, then her wide hips and thighs curved out into an arc like the bottom of a vase, and tapered suddenly into the curved tips of tiny feet.

I set the two-faced woman on the crate with the skin-suit man, and searched again in the open crate, moving the straw very gingerly until I saw dark brown clay in the shape of a deer head. I pulled the figure out. The deer head was the high elaborate headdress of an old man wearing a long cloak and huge circle earrings. The headdress looked so heavy, I could not understand how he could have supported its weight. A young woman sat in the old man's lap. She too had on a long robe and a coiled-snake headdress, almost as high as the deer, but not tilted back as precariously. She was looking benignly at the old man, and her hand was raised to his cheek. His hand was wedged between the girl's legs. On the back of the figure a mouthpiece for a reed instrument was inserted. I put my mouth to it and blew; the clay couple made a shrill whistling noise that caused the seagulls outside to flap their wings and lift off the dunes in a flock.

I set the whistling couple down and moved more straw aside in the open crate. I saw a stone arm, incised with intricate designs. I moved the straw away from the figure and pulled it out. It was another stone man, standing up. He was stiff and geometrically shaped, with a cone hat that had chevron designs etched in the headband. He wore hoop earrings and a blank expression on his face. His whole body, his skirt and shoulder pads, were tattooed with minute shapes: swirls, braids, triangles, hieroglyphs. On his back were more hieroglyphs, swirls, snakes and imprints, the back flaps of his skirt, and a quiver for arrows. Instead of hair or a smooth surface on the back of his head, the man had a second face—the face of a skeleton.

The gulls were squawking. I went to the window and looked out. The sun had moved and the shadows were slanting at shorter angles. I had no idea how long I had been rummaging in the crate. I decided I would look at one more object, and then go back. I pulled out another figure. Made from a smooth blond stone, it was a man, seated on a stone block, naked except for a huge wildcat headdress. The face of a tiger or a jaguar maybe, it had sharp triangular teeth, and a geometric shaped head with rectangular slabs for the ridges of the nose. The naked man was slouching under the headdress, and pressed his hands against the stone seat, as if to support the weight. He looked bewildered.

I put the jaguar man back into the crate in the exact spot where I had pulled him out, then padded him with straw. I put the other figures back—the skeleton man, the whistling couple, the two-faced woman—trying to figure out what each one meant. I put the lid back on the crate, and used the flat side of the crowbar to hammer the nails back in. The little skin-suit man with the dangling hand-gloves was still sitting on the other crate. I was going to take him with me.

I set out across the dunes with the skin-suit man cupped in my arm. When I reached the shoreline I followed it toward Hatches Harbor, glancing down now and then at the little man's mournful expression, his open mouth and hollow eyes. I wondered what kind of predicament he was in, why he had this peculiar outfit on. I thought if I stared at him long enough, or kept him with me, the reason would come clear. But that was an excuse to keep him. The truth was I had grown attached to him, sitting there cross-legged on the crate lid, watching me in his outrageous skin suit, while I dug out the other figures. I wondered if they were Etruscan, Minoan, Babylonian, or Indian; if they were ancient or modern, real or fake. Perhaps they were decoys to divert attention from drug smuggling and gun running, or the drugs—heroin and cocaine—were stashed inside the skeleton man and the two-faced woman, and the whistling couple. I asked myself why, if all he were smuggling were these hand-sized figures, why he had so many crates. I tried to gauge how many figurines he could have acquired. I wondered if he had looted a gravesite, robbed a palace, or retrieved the treasure in a sunken ship.

***

When I got home I lay on my side in bed holding the skin-suit man, and looked out the window at the roof tops of the east end, the bay, the outline of the coast going up-Cape. Everything looked so sweet, so dear—the light coming up, the quaint rooftops, the water shimmering, the tiny boats, the gulls. Everything looked so precious, the way it must seem to a person who has had a long illness, who might have died even, and one day he wakes up, there are fresh sheets on the bed, he is wearing a clean flannel nightshirt, and the girl next to the bed tells him he is going to pull through.

I watched a van pull up out front that had *Compton Moving and Storage* written on the side. Two young men got out of the van, and with very big wire clippers, cut through the bike cables that strapped my bike to the fence. I watched one young man pick up my bike, the cherished red three-speed Columbia I rarely rode, and hoist it into the van. I jumped off the bed. Those bastards, they were stealing my bike. Gangs from up-Cape were known to come down at dawn with their big vans and cart off as many bikes as they could get. The junkier the bike, the hipper it was, so I knew my old Columbia was a rare prize for them. Funky bikes were a valuable commodity in Key West, where the robbers took the contraband and sold it. What was hip in Provincetown was usually hip there. It was a circuit.

I felt in my jeans pocket for my car keys. I crept downstairs, opened the car door, climbed in, and peered at the thieves over the dashboard. I looked around for something to copy down the license plate with, but the bike thieves were blocking my view. Finally, they threw my neighbor's green ten-speed into the van, and I caught a glimpse of the inside. It was so full they were throwing bikes on their sides, over the tops of the bikes that were standing. The two young men jumped into the front of the van and sped off. I started the car and pulled out after them.

When they were speeding along the Cape Highway I

realized my mistake. I should have called the police first, and then followed them so they would not get away. Now I would have to follow these jerks all the way to their first stop. I wondered if they were driving to Palm Beach. Perhaps the van held tons of gas. Maybe they had prearranged stop-off points where friends were waiting. This was dangerous business. I beat on the steering wheel and turned the radio on. I was going to catch these bicycle thieves once and for all. I would be the new Town Hero.

They were approaching the rotary at Orleans. I thought I was going to lose them on the rotary. But there was no traffic to dodge, and they did not speed up and try to shake me. They probably did not even notice I was following them, in this bland mid-sized American sedan. I looked around; no other cars were on the highway. Then I spotted a Highway Patrol car parked on the side of the road ahead of me. I pulled up next to it. "Bike Thieves! Bike Thieves!" I said.

The patrolmen looked up from their clipboards. "Calm down, lady, " the driver said.

"That van stole my bike!" I said. "I saw them! The van's full of stolen bikes!"

The patrolman started his car. "You better follow me, lady," he said. He pulled out very fast, without turning on his lights or siren.

When the patrol car got close enough behind the van, its lights began to flash. The van pulled over, the highway patrol car pulled over behind them, and I followed the patrol car. By the time I was parked, the patrolman who had been driving was already questioning the driver of the van and inspecting his license. The other patrolman had circled around to the passenger side. The patrolman pointed to my car. The first bike thief leaned his head out the window and looked back at me. I smiled ruefully. I had caught that bastard.

When the two bike thieves were handcuffed in the back of the patrol car and the highway patrolman had called in the arrest on his CB radio, he walked over to my car. "Would you mind approaching the back of the van and pointing out which bikes you believe you saw the two men steal?" He had the invoices in his hand.

I walked around to the open doors of the van. "That's my bike," I said, pointing to the red one lying on its side over the top.

"And you saw them steal that one? Was it locked up?"

"To a fence," I said. "Then they stole the green one across the street." I pointed out the ten-speed. The highway patrolman could not tell which one I was pointing to, so I climbed into the van and put my hand on it. When I was about to turn around and climb down again I noticed the crates—a whole stack of them ran along the back of the van, behind the bikes. They had a tarp thrown over them. My own bike lay on top of the crates, not on the other bikes, as I had imagined, looking into the van from a distance. I recognized the crates. They were Harper's, from Hatches Harbor Light. There was no mistaking them. Even the tarp was the same. If I had left the lighthouse any later I would have met the bike thieves as they were coming in to pick up the crates.

"That's a consignment load," the highway patrolman said. I turned around. He waved the invoice in the air. "From Provincetown. It might be legit. We'll have to check it out." He wrote down my name and address while I stared into the back of the van and tried desperately to think of something to say that would prevent them from holding the crates, but I did not know what I could do. I had nowhere to put them, the van was already confiscated and the drivers arrested. What a mess I had made. The hero. Caught the bike thieves, and got Harper in a lot of trouble. The highway patrolman asked me to follow them to the station in Orleans, where I would need to fill out a report.

It was already nine in the morning when I drove from Orleans back to Provincetown, wondering how I was going to break the news to Harper. I did not want to admit I had spied on him at Hatches Harbor, but I had to warn him his crates had been confiscated. I would not admit I had opened one of the crates, or knew what was inside, or had stolen the skin-suit man.

***

Five minutes before midnight I stood at the gate in front of Raphael Souza's house and plucked a honeysuckle blossom off the vine that was intertwined in the wire fence, crushed the blossom in my fingers and smelled it. The flags had been taken down from the mast. The sheepdog Zac stood on the porch and barked perfunctorily, but did not run at me or jump on me when I approached him, whispering and cooing the way Lydia did her parrot Sydney Greenstreet. I looked up at the windows to see which ones were lit. The house looked just as mysterious from inside the gate as it had from outside.

I walked up the stairs to the front entrance and patted Zac on the head. "Good dog," I said. When I had convinced Zac that I was someone he had known for years, I started around to the back of the house. Zac trotted after me. I slipped through some bushes, passed underneath a plaster of a woman carrying an urn on her shoulder, and an archer pulling his bow taut, ready to let an arrow fly. The kitchen door was unlocked. Zac climbed up the stairs with me and whimpered to be let in. "You have to stay outside and guard the house," I said to him. "Go on, get back." Zac trotted down the stairs and sat on the lawn whining. I let myself in.

The house was dark, so I felt my way through the kitchen into the entrance hall, which was lit. Except for the hardwood floors, which had ornate Persian rugs thrown over them, the house was just as white inside as out. The entrance hall gave way to a large living room beyond it and a vast window on the back wall made of diamond-shaped beveled panes. On either side of the entryway a white staircase led up to the second floor. I searched the walls under the stairways for any doors that might lead to the cupola.

The upstairs hallway was narrow and gloomy, lit only by a few dim candelabra lights on the walls. A series of shut doors faced the balcony railing. I was convinced that one of them must lead to the cupola. A waist high mahogany credenza with glass doors and a malachite top sat against the wall between the first and second doors. A ceramic vase with raised images of a woman's back, and imitation red and black Attica vases of naked men wrestling were displayed inside the credenza. I continued down the hallway, passing a copy of *The Repulse of Atilla* in an arched frame.

Finally, I opened the last door. The bedroom walls were covered with bronze mirrors. In one corner of the room a wooden armoire reached the ceiling. Its doors were decorated with griffins inlaid in cherry wood, brandishing their claws at each other, like lions in an old family crest. The bed was covered with a down quilt. A W.C. Fields doll was pinned to the wall over the bed where the crucifix should have hung; a box of cigars sat on the floor underneath it. Across from the bed sat a simple walnut dresser with models of schooners displayed on top.

I searched the room for the stairs to the cupola. I did not see them, so I started opening doors. The first one went to the bathroom. I opened another door; it was a closet full of jeans, shirts and leather jackets that gave off a lemony scent of Yves Saint Laurent cologne.

Since there were no more doors, I opened the armoire. The clothes in there were bigger and darker colored, and smelled of cigars and Paco Rabanne. I pushed some hangers down the rack so I could inspect a leather flight jacket. The guys looked good in these. When I pushed the clothes away I noticed the armoire did not have a back, and there was no bronze mirrored wall behind it. When I stepped through the opening and stood up, like Alice, stepping through the rabbit hole into Wonderland, I was at the bottom of a steep, narrow stairway, the kind that led up to an attic—or a cupola.

I slid my hands along the walls to keep my balance while I climbed the steep stairs. When I reached the top I was in a little box, with windows on all four sides, and wooden benches built in beneath the windows. I sat down on the nearest bench. Harper was sitting across from me, dressed in his usual outfit: the beige chinos, white shirt, string tie, leather jacket, fedora, and wing tips. He had a letter-sized envelope in his hand. "How did you expect me to find this place?" I said.

"You can see it from the street," he said, pointing over

his shoulder. I looked out the windows. Crowds of people on the street wandered in and out of bars, beyond them lay the shiny expanse of bay, the lighthouses and breakwater, the moored boats.

"Listen, babe," he said. "The cops picked up the last load of merchandise for my company. The movers I hired turned out to be bicycle thieves. Anyway, the cops are suspicious about the merchandise, and they're sore they can't find me so—"

"Why don't you talk to them? Is the merchandise stolen?"

"No, it's all completely on the level. But I'm afraid they'll throw me in the slammer anyway. So listen, this is what you have to do. Take this envelope down to New York City. There's a driver waiting for you outside. If the cops here give my merchandise to the Feds then you—"

"But why would they give your merchandise to the Feds if it's not stolen?"

"It didn't go through Customs, that's why. Now listen, if the cops here give my merchandise to the Feds, my art dealer will contact you in New York, and then you deliver this envelope to Dan Rather at the CBS Evening News." He handed me the envelope. It was sealed and on the front was typed, *DAN RATHER, MANAGING EDITOR, THE CBS EVENING NEWS.*

"You have to deliver it in person," he said. "Straight to Dan Rather. No intermediaries. Your hands to his hands. Is it a deal?"

"But Harper, we're talking about *Dan Rather.* They're not going to let me in to see *Dan Rather.* Are you kidding? That's like making an appointment with the President, or requesting an audience with the Pope."

"Don't be a sucker. Dan Rather is a regular guy, like you and me. He has a wife and kids; he plays golf on the weekends. Now be a sport. Give him the envelope. Just tell them you have confidential information on the Federal customs inspection case in Hyannis, and they'll let you see him. Trust me."

"Jesus Christ Harper, we're talking about *Dan Rather*," I repeated.

"Go on down now. Don't be a dope. I haven't got much time, and the driver's waiting for you. And thanks, babe."

I walked halfway down the stairs and came back again. "Harper, if it's just a Customs violation, why don't you turn yourself in?"

"It might escalate. I've got other people to protect. I want them to agree to some terms first."

"You sound like a hijacker."

"That's right. Now get out of here. We're running late."

"But why would it escalate if the merchandise isn't stolen?"

"It's all in the statement. You'll hear it on the *CBS Evening News*. Maybe in a special report. Now get lost. Blow this joint."

I started down the stairs and came back again. "Harper?" I said. "I have to tell you something before you go."

"Quick then."

"I was the one who arrested the bike thieves."

Harper started laughing. "*You*?"

"I didn't know your merchandise was in there. I was up all night, in the morning I saw this van parked outside my house, and they were stealing my bike, so I jumped into my car and I—"

"Kate, Kate, tell me some other time."

"I'm really sorry Harper, I had no idea—"

"It's not your fault, Kate, really."

I went down the stairs. I stopped at the bottom and turned around to go up again. I wanted to confess everything, that I had been spying on him at the Ice House, that I had found the crates at Hatches Harbor Light and opened one, that I had stolen the skin-suit man. But the room seemed to be vibrating and I felt like I needed air, so I pushed my way through the armoire, ran downstairs and let myself out the kitchen door. I crept past the statues, through the bushes and across the lawn. When I reached the gate I looked around to see if anyone noticed me, but the wind gusted suddenly and the humming and shuddering intensified like the ominous noise before an earthquake. Everyone on Commercial Street had stopped and was looking up at the sky. I looked up too. A helicopter hovered above Raphael Souza's house, and a man was climbing up a rope ladder hanging from the helicopter down to Souza's roof. It was Harper of course—I recognized the fedora. Two men in the body of the helicopter crouched down over the door and pulled him in. They brought up the rope and shut the door. The helicopter flew away.

"It's like *Apocalypse Now*," a bystander said.

Someone pulled on my arm. "I'm the driver," a voice said. I wheeled around. It was Gabriel Paradise.

Chapter Two

Monday—one week later

All of Provincetown was in an uproar. The Law Offices of Ruth Allen Esq. had established the *Harper Martin Defense Fund*, and everyone in town was planning benefits or parties, contests or shows, to raise money for the Fund. Raphael Souza had announced a costume party at the White Sands, all proceeds from liquor sales and cover charges would go to the Harper Martin Defense Fund. Paradiso's was sponsoring a New Wave Night for Harper; Paula and Christianne's show that evening would also be a benefit for the Fund. Dominic was planning to stage a windsurfing regatta off the wharf at Cosmo's restaurant; all entry fees and liquor sales that afternoon would be donated to the Harper Martin Defense Fund. Antaeus had authorized Joe Houston to give a benefit screening of *The Rocky Horror Picture Show* at the Bad Attitude Cinema. Edward the real estate agent planned to give a tour of all the Historical

Plaque Houses in town, and donate the fees to the Defense Fund. Grace was raffling off a djellaba from her store, in conjunction with Slashette's *Fashion Espionage Show*, held at the Djellaba store, in which Slashette and the other cocktail waitresses at the Bad Attitude would be the models. All raffle and ticket money would be donated to the Harper Martin Defense Fund. Animus Pizza was sponsoring a Bocce Tournament, all entry fees and concession money that day to be donated. Joshua was organizing a Karate show to be staged in front of Town Hall. Angelo was sponsoring a benefit Whale watch, all ticket sales would go to the fund. And finally, the opening of Antaeus' gallery, featuring Cosmo's new paintings, would be a benefit for the Harper Martin Defense Fund. All liquor sales would be donated to the fund. Antaeus' appeal for a liquor license for the new gallery had been granted, swept along on a wave of community solidarity engendered by the Harper Martin Defense.

Harper Martin was not in jail yet; he was still at large. The Federal subpoena issued for his arrest was for questioning only, in regard to possible U.S. Trade and Customs violations on imported goods. But after everyone heard Dan Rather read Harper's statement on the *CBS Evening News*, Ruth and the investors for Maniac Drifter Inc. thought it would be wise to start the Defense Fund right away, to cultivate community spirit and participation during the upcoming media coverage, and to have the money ready at a moment's notice, if Harper did turn himself in, and the Federal government did decide to prosecute.

Gabriel Paradise had installed his television in the Land Ho, so the Cosmo's restaurant workers could rush in and watch the *CBS Evening News* when Dan Rather gave his

"Temple of the Jaguars Report." Cosmo had brought his own TV into the front dining room of the restaurant, because the customers wanted to watch the news. All the bars and restaurants in town had their TVs tuned to the *CBS Evening News* for the Temple of the Jaguars Report. The bars were getting more and more crowded every day, as people got hooked on the story and wanted to hear his report. The Happy Hour business was booming. It seemed the entire nation was addicted to the daily updates, and the *CBS Evening News* ratings were skyrocketing.

Everyone in Provincetown had watched the very first broadcast, when Dan Rather had read Harper's statement. The locals had been waiting for the broadcast for 24 hours, ever since an anonymous caller had tipped off the *Provincetown Express*. Gabe and I were relieved, since we wanted everyone to watch the broadcast, but did not want me to be revealed as the Informant.

The delivery had come off without a hitch. Harper's art dealer contacted Gabe and me when the Federal agents took possession of the crates. Gabe drove me to the CBS offices in midtown Manhattan; somehow I convinced the front desk of the urgency and secrecy of the information, and I had been granted an audience with Dan Rather himself. I could not believe it.

Now I was the Informant. I was the *Anonymous Source who had informed CBS News* etc., etc. I tried not to smile whenever I heard Mr. Rather use that expression. All the television viewers, in Provincetown and around the nation, and sometimes in magazine and newspaper editorials on the story, were calling the informant *Deep Throat* after the informant in the Watergate Scandal. Deep Throat's identity had never been revealed, even though the government had asked journalists over and over through the years to reveal their sources, had their papers, tapes and filed subpoenaed, held them in contempt of court, and even thrown them in jail. But nobody in the Federal Government had asked Dan Rather to identify his informant. Everybody said Dan would never reveal his sources. He was the American Journalist of the Hour, like Cronkite during Vietnam, like Woodard and Bernstein during Watergate, like I.F. Stone and Walter Lippmann in their day. He was a National Hero.

On the very first broadcast, Dan Rather had read Harper's letter on the national news. It had started out, *Dear Mr. Dan Rather,* and had gone on to explain that Harper was a painter who showed his work frequently in Manhattan, and had recently gone into business as an art dealer who specialized in Ancient Art, rare or precious art objects from ancient cultures in Africa, Egypt, Greece, Asia, Oceania, Central and South America. The reaction in Provincetown was: "Since when did he become an art dealer?" And: "Where's Oceania?"

The letter went on to say that Harper had made a trip to Nicaragua the previous winter, and during his stay there had purchased the moveable remains of a recently excavated Classic Mayan temple called *The Temple of the Jaguars.* The objects included: stone stela depicting the ruler-deities Jaguar Snake, Bird Jaguar, Shield Jaguar and other god impersonators; door lintels—limestone relief carving depicting visionary and penitential rites including bloodletting, rites of fertility and mythical events, rattlesnakes swallowing human skeletons; a serpent mask doorway that had teeth lining the sill, fangs protruding from the jambs, and the serpent's nose and eyes above—(the doorway was the serpent's gullet, and a line of human heads decorated the cornice); a jaguar throne made of painted red stone inlaid with jade; an illustrated screenfold manuscript, similar to the ones displayed in Paris, Dresden and Madrid, on paper made from wild fig bark and sealed with lime coating, depicting the passage into the underworld of the twin deities of the Popol Vuh; clay and stone figurines (including replicas of the fertility god Xipe Totec, earth Goddess Catlicue, figures representing the prankster-spirit chanenques; a representation of Tlacolteotl, Goddess of Dirt, stegapygous figures; shell, spider and turtle shell men; a spider monkey dancing on a human head, and other figures); painted clay pottery mixed with volcanic ash, and painted with orange or white slip, depicting bat gods, desert foxes, and the three headed crocodile deity; a detailed plan of the designs on the hieroglyphic stairway leading to the Temple of the Jaguars, the general layout of the buildings around the temple including the Steam Bath, Ball Court, Pyramid of the Magician, House of the Governor, High Priest's Grave, Skull Platform, Castille, Mercado and Akab Dzib, and a complete outline of the Jaguar Mural; full round freestanding stucco portrait heads; jade carvings; effigy pendants of condors, pumas, armadillos, lobsters and monsters with crocodile heads on human bodies; funerary masks made from pottery, basalt, onyx, jadeite and obsidian; small hematite mirrors; stone vessels made in the shape of a hyena, and an organ cactus, killer whale, coyote; effigy vessels depicting iguanas, crustaceans, and molluscs.

Harper had said in his statement that he had purchased the pieces from the Temple of the Jaguars from the Nicaraguan government, after having agreed to certain terms.

The terms were that a replica of the temple would be erected to house the art objects and artifacts, that all the art objects would be housed in the temple replica, that no objects would be sold or distributed separately. It was also stipulated that Harper Martin himself would recreate the great Jaguar Mural, similar to the twelve-wall mural that covered three rooms in the famous Bonampak Temple in Guatemala. The Nicaraguan government agreed that the purchaser of the temple art objects would not be obliged to recreate the pyramid that supported the temple, nor the series of shafts, vaults, tombs, and crypts inside the pyramid, but a diagram of the pyramid, and a sketch of the surrounding buildings, should be made available to the visitors of the temple replica.

The statement went on to say that Harper had purchased the temple art objects with a down payment of IBM computers, which were shipped to Nicaragua by private boat from California, in order to avoid possible federal intervention through U.S. Customs Inspection. Here, Dan interrupted his reading to explain that since we were aiding rebels fighting the Sandinista government of Nicaragua, the U.S.A. had instituted trade sanctions against Nicaragua, and U.S. citizens were not allowed any commerce with them. The statement went on to say that Harper had paid the balance of the purchase price upon receipt of the merchandise in Provincetown.

After purchasing the temple art objects, Harper shipped the artifacts to Provincetown, again avoiding U.S. Customs for the same reasons, and stored the artifacts in Provincetown until his dealer in Manhattan sold them to the new J. Paul Getty Museum in Malibu, California. The Getty Museum purchased the art objects for an undisclosed price, and agreed to the terms of sale set forth by the Nicaraguan government. The Getty Foundation planned to erect the Temple replica on the site of the new museum, in the Malibu hills just outside of Los Angeles, overlooking the Pacific Ocean.

Harper's statement said he was willing and able to pay all import taxes to the Federal Government, provide them with a complete accounting of all art objects purchased, pay any necessary fines or serve any necessary jail terms for customs violations, if the Federal Government would agree to two conditions: 1. to release the confiscated merchandise (crates containing the figurines) to the Getty Museum so the terms of sale could be honored; and, 2. to agree not to prosecute any associates in the sale, including the art dealer, boat crews, investors of Maniac Drifter Inc., informants, or representatives of the Getty Museum.

Harper's letter finished by declaring that none of the shippers or investors had any knowledge of the nature of the operation, nor did the Art Dealer or Getty Museum have any knowledge of the U.S. Trade or Customs violations. He went on to say that he had avoided Customs because he knew that the political relations between the United States and Nicaraguan governments were not friendly, understood we had a trade embargo against that country, and feared the U.S. Government would confiscate the art objects and prevent the sale.

When Dan Rather had finished reading the letter, he thanked his television viewers for listening, and promised to have more information about the Temple of the Jaguars story in his next broadcast. "And that's the CBS News for Wednesday, July 10, 1985. I'm Dan Rather. Goodnight." The camera pulled back, showing the newsroom, the tickertape noise erupted, and you could see Dan Rather looking thoughtful and earnest, as he folded up Harper's letter.

The broadcasts over the next few days had focused on various aspects of the temple and U.S.-Nicaraguan relations. CBS reporters visited the Getty Museum, and filmed the opening of the crates they did possess, showing glimpses of the serpent mask doorframes, some painted pottery, a stucco head. CBS graphics experts provided artists' renderings of what the Temple of the Jaguars might look like if recreated on the Getty Museum site in Malibu, and what it might have looked like during the Late Classic Mayan Period.

Reporters travelled to Nicaragua, to report on the new government since Somoza, and the U.S.-backed Contra rebellion. They showed the Nicaraguan government agencies learning to use their new computers with the help of American volunteers. Archaeologists and Mayan specialists were called in to explain the background and history of the artifacts in the possession of the Getty Museum, and to speculate on the nature of the figurines confiscated by the U.S. Government. Representatives of the governments in Guatemala and Honduras issued statements that the Nicaraguan temple was a hoax, that the Mayans never ventured as far south as Nicaragua, and that Harper Martin and the Getty Museum had been duped into selling Nicaragua computers and giving them millions in American dollars. Another broadcast showed how visits to the existing Getty Museum in Malibu had quadrupled even though the Temple of the Jaguars would not be finished for at least a month and the art objects could not be exhibited until the temple replica was complete, in keeping with the terms of purchase.

Dan concluded by saying that Harper Martin was still at

large. His subpoena was still out for questioning regarding U.S. Customs violations. The Federal government had not responded to Harper's statement, and refused to comment. Then Dan promised to have a complete update on the government position as soon as it was forthcoming, complete coverage of Benefit Week in Provincetown, and a profile of Harper Martin in upcoming reports. Gabe and I were getting along much better since our trip to New York. Gabe forgave me for the nights when I slept with Getz, and Joe, and the night I had driven Mary to Boston. Since he had driven me to New York we had not been apart. Now it was Monday, and the week of benefit parties, races, tournaments, fashion shows and cabarets for the Harper Martin Defense Fund was about to begin.

***

The bouncer for the Harper Martin Defense Fund Benefit Costume Ball at the White Sands was dressed as a giant squid. The costume consisted of a flesh colored leotard with lavender blotches on it. The tentacles emerged at his shoulders—big, stuffed arms made of the same pinkish fabric and painted with blotches, like a rag doll gone berserk. He wore a hood over his head, with bug eyes made of balls that were covered with silver glitter and stuck out from the hood, and in his hand, hidden under the tentacles, he held a squirt gun that let loose an indigo fluid.

I walked into the party singing *"Romance Without Finance is a Nuisance."* I was dressed very simply in a pair of beige chinos, a white tailored shirt, black string tie, leather jacket, black socks and wing tips, with my long blond hair swept up into my fedora. I swaggered around talking like the Continental Op, and coughed on an unfiltered Camel cigarette. I went up to the bar where Uncle Sam, dressed in a top hat adorned with American flag, blue tails, a white shirt, and red and white striped pants, was talking to a seven-foot tall cardboard replica of the Empire State Building, with all its windows etched in, and the tapered top of the building lovingly rendered so it narrowed slowly to a point. "I wanted to come as a phallic symbol," the Empire State Building was telling Uncle Sam, "so my friend said to me: Why not the Empire State Building? Don't you think it was a good idea?"

"You should get together with this guy," Uncle Sam said, pointing at the bartender, who was dressed as King Kong. "All you need now is Faye Wray."

I ordered a club soda with lime from King Kong and turned around to look at the dance floor. A lithe young woman dressed as a Turkish belly dancer took up most of the space. Guys in white togas with wreaths around their heads were also out on the dance floor, some men from the Rescue Squad and volunteer fire department had arrived wearing their uniforms. The Three Muses, men dressed in powder blue silk strapless dresses, with white veils and feathered headdresses, were performing a ring dance, waving their gold wands in the air. A transvestite was dressed up like Liza Minnelli in *Cabaret*, in a black backless V-neck body suit with black tights, fishnet stockings and stiletto heels.

Some of the people were dressed up in Aztec and Mayan outfits, probably influenced by Dan Rather's *CBS Special Report on Pre-Columbian Art—An Overview* that aired the week before as part of the series for the Temple of the Jaguars Story. One guy was dressed like Catlicue, the decapitated Aztec earth goddess, with a necklace of rattlesnake heads around his skirt, and a double cobra mask over his head. Some people wore falcon headdresses and killer whale headdresses, like the Nazca's wore. In his *CBS Special Report on Pre-Columbian Art*, Dan Rather had explained that these costumes were part of an imitative magic. If a warrior painted his eyes with falcon markings, his vision would be as sharp as a falcon's. If a fisherman wore the symbols of a serrated mouth and dorsal fin of the killer whale, he would be as swift as the whale. The costumes allowed the warrior or fisherman to take on the special qualities of these animals, who were also believed to be gods.

A sleek, muscled boy was out on the dance floor, skateboarding in circles and pirouettes around the Turkish Belly Dancer. He was shirtless, with the top two buttons of his fatigue pants undone, and he wore a huge paper maché mask of the Extra Terrestrial over his head. The ET mask looked exactly like the character in the Lucas-Spielberg movie: with its bug eyes, brown wrinkled skin, receding chin and baleful, puppy-dog expression.

A person wearing a Fox head and another person wearing an Alligator head sat down on either side of me. "How was the Dyke Dinner?" the Alligator said. It was Nichole's voice.

Nichole was Cosmo's daughter. She was a painter at Days Studio and a friend of mine. She had gotten me a job at Cosmo's restaurant. But she was mad at me for three reasons:

First, I had taken our mutual friend Whitney, who was also a painter, to Paradiso's to hear Christianne sing.

Whitney met a silver-haired lesbian there named Elaine, who looked like Lauren Bacall. Now they were lovers.

Second, I had driven my friend Mary, who was also a lesbian and a bartender at Paradiso's, to Boston to see her mother, who was dying of cancer. Nichole was a local. The locals didn't like the gays.

Third, Nichole had taken up with a married carpenter named Frank, and her father Cosmo disapproved. Nichole thought I took her father's side in the argument.

"So how was the Dyke Dinner?" Nichole repeated.

"Elaine Barry made the best paella I ever tasted."

"Did you see Harper make his Great Escape from the Souza's cupola to the helicopter, under the watchful eye of three thousand people?"

"I saw it from the street."

"I thought it was a little staged myself," she said through the Alligator head. "Elaine and Whitney must have thought there was an earthquake."

"I didn't see them around; maybe they were at Paradiso's."

"Figures," she said. "You didn't go with them? That's a relief. How's *your* lesbian?"

"She's not mine and she's in Boston," I said.

"So you're here slumming it with the underage boys, the faggots, the Harper Martin cult and the new Pre-Columbian fashion craze, huh?"

"It may be the biggest thing since the post-apocalyptic Mad Max clothes," I said.

"I hear Pierre Cardin is coming out with a Temple of the Jaguars Collection for this fall. There's a fashion preview in Paris in a few days."

"Jesus Christ," I said.

"Exactly. It's cult of personality: the President's jelly-bean craze, Beatle-mania, *The Sufferings of Young Werther.*"

"Speak of the devil," Frank said through his fox mask. Four gay men walked by them, dressed as owl man, crab man, spider man, and turtle-shell man respectively, as had been described in the CBS Special Report.

"The gays weren't into this Pre-Columbian paraphernalia until Dan Rather had to tell them that the Mohicans painted pictures of masturbation, sodomy, and people strapped to their beds onto their pottery," Nichole said.

"Did he really say that, on national television?" I said.

"He was delicate," she said. "He said they might have conveyed the concepts of divine inspiration, afflatus and possession. It was in Harper's statement, part of the temple artifacts."

"Look," Frank said, "more people dressed up like Harper Martin." He pointed to the bar and dance floor. The two guys by the bar, talking to King Kong, had on the requisite chinos, leather jackets string ties and fedoras. The guy at the edge of the dance floor was wearing a brown fedora, a safari shirt, blue jeans, boots, and held a whip in his hands.

"That one by the dance floor isn't Harper Martin," I said. "That one is Harrison Ford playing Indiana Jones in *The Temple of Doom.*"

Whitney and Elaine were standing at the door, talking to the Giant Squid. Whitney was dressed as a cat burglar, in black tights, and tunic, a black mask, high top tennis shoes, a coiled rope and a sack thrown over her shoulder. Elaine was dressed as Lauren Bacall in *To Have and Have Not*, in a 1940s Coco Chanel tailored suit with wide lapels, padded shoulders and oversized buttons, and carrying a black patent leather handbag. Whitney was admiring the Giant Squid, inspecting his tentacles, and running her fingers along the lavender blotches. Whitney loved colors. Elaine took a pack of Player's from her patent leather bag and lit one. She looked around, saw me, and lifted her cigarette to me. Whitney noticed too, waved, and they started over.

"It's the dykes," Nichole said. "This is where we exit. Want to dance, Frank?" They went off and blended into the crowd. They had positioned themselves near the Turkish Belly Dancer and Extra Terrestrial when Whitney and Elaine sat down with me. "So who's the Alligator and the Fox?" Whitney said.

"They're traveling incognito," I said. "What's in the sack?"

"Paint rags."

"Some burglar," I said. "Aren't you supposed to climb over rooftops and steal jewels, like in *To Catch a Thief* with Cary Grant and Grace Kelly?"

We sat there for a while and watched the people come in. Grace arrived in a gray and orange striped djellaba from her store. Getz and Dominic arrived in their wet suits. The Mother of the Year showed up in the Voodoo Woman's leopard outfit. The Voodoo Woman was wearing layers of white pull over blouses and gathered skirts, a black turban on her head, and black rings around her eyes.

"So why won't Nichole talk to me?" Whitney said.

"What?" I said.

"The Alligator and the Fox. What—do you think I'm blind?"

"She was trying to spare your feelings," Elaine said.

Joe sauntered over in his Indiana Jones costume, set his

coiled whip down on the bench and pulled two magazines out of the back pocket of his blue jeans.

Joe usually wore tight black short-shorts, and a black t-shirt that had *Bad Attitude* emblazoned in magenta script just above the right breast pocket. He wore his pack of Gauloises rolled up into his right sleeve. Joe also wore a black glove on his left hand. He used the gloved hand at the Bad Attitude Cinema to slow the uptake reel when the film slipped off and sent it spinning. At first he only wore it in the projection room, but after awhile this became his trademark and he never took it off. The morning I woke up in bed with him he was wearing the black glove. At the time, I checked myself for cuts and bruises, but I didn't have any. I also inspected the glove. It had no buckles, snaps or clips. The seams were sewn on the inside so the edges were smooth. The fingers were cut out of the top, like racing gloves. I tried to remember if he had worn the glove all evening or if he had put it back on right before he went to sleep. I had wondered if this were his trademark in bed as well as the Cinema, and on the streets, and if so what the innovation was. But of course I couldn't remember.

Joe also worked at Animus Pizza, across from Paradiso's. I bought my chocolate egg cream there each day. He took pride in making it for me, and always made sure it had a luxurious head of foam on it. He often stood there admiring it, before he sold it to me. Joe had sandy hair in a short brush cut, tawny skin, and as Ruth had remarked, a nice build.

"Look, Kate," he said, showing me the magazines. "AIDS made it to the cover of both *Time* and *Newsweek*, and there's even an inset photo of Rock Hudson on the *Newsweek*."

"I wondered when that whole story was going to break," I said. "Gay men have had the disease for five years, but it doesn't make the cover of *Time* until an actor gets it."

"You can't get it from saliva," Whitney said. "But I hear you can get it from tears."

We looked at the magazines, which showed the virus under a microscope, some of the cadaverous patients, the research laboratories, graphs and statistics of how many people had contracted the disease and the percentage of those who had died. They showed one family in which the husband had given it to the wife, the wife to their baby in the womb, so their three-year-old daughter was the only one who didn't have it. She would be an orphan within a few years.

"This epidemic is going to ruin anorexia as a fashion," Joe said. "Look how skeletal these people are."

"It really wastes you," Whitney said. "I wish they'd find a vaccine."

"It's like syphilis in Europe in the 19th century," I said. "Everyone was dying of it, no one would talk about it. After awhile syphilis was the leading cause of death there."

"And to think, all they needed was some penicillin," Elaine said. "Since gays have it they think it's the Wrath of God or something."

"They thought the Plague was the Wrath of God," Joe said.

"That was the Age of Darkness," Whitney said.

"Welcome to the 20th century," Joe said.

"I never thought this would upset you, Joe," Elaine said.

"I'm a mysterious guy," Joe said, winking. Then he put his hat over his heart and said to me: "Would you and

Whitney and Nichole be willing to judge the Bocce Tournament on Wednesday at Animus Pizza? It's for the Harper Martin Defense Fund."

Whitney and I looked at each other. "I don't see why not," I said. "I'll tell Nichole."

"Wednesday afternoon at Animus Pizza," Joe said.

"We'll be there," Whitney said. Then she and Elaine ran off to dance. Whitney carried her sack with her, and kept bumping it against people's shoulders. She tried to edge closer and closer to the Fox and the Alligator, but Elaine kept pulling her away.

Joe and I watched from the bench. Men in jumpsuits were unraveling cable along the edges of the dance floor, erecting tripods and clamping spotlights on them. Other men hoisted video cameras on their shoulders, carried microphones and worked their way onto the dance floor, pointing the cameras and microphones at the Giant Squid and the Turkish Belly Dancer. Another one headed for the bar, where he attempted to interview the Empire State Building.

"They've arrived," Joe said, motioning with his hand at the camera crews.

"I see that," I said.

"So do you miss me?" he said, kissing my ear. I looked at him, startled. "What?" he said. "You look like you saw a ghost."

I patted his knee. "I thought I remembered something," I said.

"Do I remind you of someone you used to know?"

"Maybe," I said.

"The shadow of my former self perhaps?" I laughed. "You just miss me. You need another dose." He kissed my ear again and whispered into it: "I know your weaknesses. I'll be there." Then he got up, picked the whip up off the bench and strapped it through his belt loop. "Later," he said. "For now I have to drop down into the snake pit in order to retrieve the volcanic rock that preserves life, brings rain and restores the harvest to the villagers. Isn't that the plot-line of that stupid movie?"

"Sequels are never any good," I said.

Joe returned to his station at the edge of the dance floor and watched the Extra Terrestrial court the Turkish Belly Dancer. Getz sat down beside me and positioned his scotch glass on the bench between us. "Aren't you hot in that," I said, fingering the wetsuit.

"A little," he said, unzipping it. "This better?"

I smiled ruefully. Getz had one of the nicest bodies I had ever seen, and he knew I thought so, the devil. "You haven't been out lobstering lately."

He picked his scotch up off the bench, swirled the swizzle stick around in the short glass, and poked at the twist. "That's over." He cracked a smile and his eyes twinkled.

"What?"

"I can't tell you more. You might be a cop or something."

He looked up from his drink and caught my eye, then stared at me for a long time, until I ached all over. I wished I could remember the nighttime. I thought he must be the sweetest, the tenderest, the one who drove me crazy. But I didn't know. I guessed it from the way I felt when he sat close to me. It was as if I knew something about him, as if I could remember, not the details, but the way he made me feel. I shook out my arms and legs like someone who has been immobile too long and has let his limbs go to sleep.

"A lot of things are different now," he said. He was watching Indiana Jones watch the Extra Terrestrial and the Turkish Belly Dancer enact their courting ritual on the dance floor.

He wandered off in the direction of the dance floor. He stood at the edge talking to the two men dressed like Harper Martin. Dominic was dancing with the Turkish Belly Dancer now; Indiana Jones and Getz were watching; the Extra Terrestrial circled the circumference of the dance floor like a security guard at a high school senior prom.

Lance came in dressed as Yul Brenner in *The King and I*, in gold lamé balloon knickers, an embroidered vest, and gold sequined slippers. He had painted on slanted eyebrows and wore a hoop earring in one ear. I worked with Lance at Cosmo's restaurant. He was accompanied this evening by a Giant Lobster. The lobster was a deep rose madder, with black and rust specks on its claws and tail. Its claws were huge, made out of padded cloth like boxing gloves, and its chest was padded with a shield like a suit of armor. The lobster's head reached way up past the man inside's head, with a hole cut underneath for his face to peer out. At the crown of the lobster head were the bug eyes and tentacles.

Lanced walked up to me and bowed. "Shall we dance?"

"Very funny," I said.

He sat down beside me. "Would you refuse the King of Siam?" He pointed to the Giant Lobster. "That guy must be broiling."

I glared at him. "Who is that guy?"

"Wouldn't you like to know. Look at you, giving him

the hairy eyeball like that. You oughta be ashamed." We turned our attention to the side of the dance floor where some of the revelers seemed to be fighting with the cameramen. The dance music went off. When the crowd stepped back, Lance and I could see the Voodoo Woman in her layered scarf outfit, with snake bracelets around her arms and legs, and the turban on her head. She was wailing some song that sounded like an Egyptian dirge, in hard, metallic syllables, and a foreign accent. At the same time she was rattling a gourd, fiddling with a chain of beads in her and, and hopping around the cameramen.

"Look at her," Lance said, pointing to the Voodoo Woman. "She's doing some Hindu-Yuppie-Hopi-Moonie-Krishnamurti-Matahari dance to ward off the spread of AIDS to heterosexuals."

"It looks like she's trying to put a hex on the reporters," I said.

The Voodoo Woman stopped dancing and bowed, and the disco music went on again. The reporters asked the Extra Terrestrial if the Voodoo Woman were performing some ritual Mayan dance. E.T. said he didn't know anything about it.

"She just wants to get on Dan Rather's Temple of the Jaguar Report," he said. "Everyone does." Lance saw Whitney pull Elaine off the dance floor and head toward us. "The clam stuffers," he said. "Be back later"—and he was off to the bar.

Whitney sat down next to me, slung her bag off her shoulder and settled it between her feet. She pulled her eye mask off. "Tell me why Nichole won't talk to me," she said, pointing to the Alligator and the Fox on the dance floor.

"You know why," Elaine said. Then to me: "I told her why."

"I want to hear it from Kate," Whitney said. "I want to hear it from a neutral third party."

I did not want to tell Whitney what she already knew. It would only hurt her to hear it straight. It was like Gabe telling me that my inability to make a commitment was just an excuse for my sleeping around. I knew I slept around. Gabe knew it; Joe knew it; everyone knew it. But it still hurt me to hear Gabe draw conclusions about it.

"Nichole won't talk to you because you have a girlfriend," I said.

"Okay?" Elaine said. "Now you've heard someone else say it."

"But she's breaking up a marriage," Whitney said. "She's affecting other people. This is my own private matter."

"Not in Provincetown," Elaine said. "Nothing's private."

"She told you at the Bad Attitude," I said. "Remember the Polish joke?"

"Yeah," Whitney said. "What she's doing is immoral, but what I'm doing is sick." Whitney kicked the bag of paint rags at her feet. "I remember. I thought she was just joking around, giving me a hard time, trying to get the upper hand so I wouldn't come down on her about Frank. You know, jockeying for position, painter to painter."

"Oh, is that how it works?" Elaine said, lighting a Player.

"I told you at the beginning this gay stuff upsets her," I said. "She was born here. She takes everything that happens here personally."

"So I've lost a friend because of my private life? I take that personally."

"Is she really your friend if she'd drop you for that reason?" Elaine said.

Whitney looked at her. "She's really my friend," she said. "She's just screwed up in the head, that's all. Too much gesso and turpentine. It creeps up on you and then all of a sudden it attacks. You're afflicted."

"Sounds like love," I said, patting her on the shoulder.

Elaine sat down next to Whitney. "You're too generous," she said. "Now you're paying for it." Whitney leaned against her and shrugged.

Someone tapped me on the shoulder from behind. I turned around. It was the Giant Lobster. "Would you like to dance?" he said.

The dance floor was humid and close; it had that thick, claustrophobic feeling of a swamp or bayou. The Voodoo Woman was dancing with the Mother of the Year, running her braceleted arms up and down the Mother's sleek thighs. The Liza Minnelli transvestite was dancing with Uncle Sam; when he shook his head the sweat flew off his hair and spotted Uncle Sam's top hat. Lance was dancing with Grace, and was trying to climb inside her djellaba, but she kept batting him away. Nichole was next to me on the dance floor. I grabbed her arm. "So what's going on?"

Nichole looked at me through the eyeholes in her Alligator head. "You mean with Frank?"

I nodded. "He and his wife are negotiating," she said. "Like Harper Martin and the Feds."

"Joe wants us to Judge the Bocce Tournament Wednesday afternoon at Animus. Can you make it? Whitney and I said we would."

"Whitney's a dyke."

"Come on, Nichole. Whitney and I are judging the Bocce Tournament. If you want to join us, show up."

"My dad will probably be there anyway."

"You can't spend your entire life avoiding your father," I shouted.

"Can't I?" she said, took Frank's arm and led him off to the far end of the dance floor.

I looked around the floor. It seemed like it was getting even hotter, there was less and less air, and everyone was moving in tandem, without even being aware of it. While Getz and Dominic watched from the sidelines, Joe was taking his turn now with the Turkish Belly Dancer. Joe stayed close and, while the belly dancer slithered around, he wrapped her, very carefully, in his whip, until it was crossed in elaborate patterns over her veils. Lance had succeeded in getting inside Grace's djellaba with her, and she was trying to pull it over his head to get him out again. Joshua was circulating among a group of Harper Martin look-alikes, a group that had grown so large I wondered if perhaps they were a hockey team come to look in on the fun, or if a cult was actually forming.

"Can you take yourself off scan for a minute and talk to me?" the Giant Lobster said.

"I'm sorry," I said. Joshua skated up to me with a Sherman in his hand.

"Gotta Light?" he said. I shook my head. "I thought you always had a light," he said. "I thought you kept one hidden." He skated off into the crowd.

Someone put his arms around me from behind. He felt familiar. I turned around and buried my face in Getz's warm neck, until I could feel his pulse against the bridge of my nose. I shut my eyes and put my hand in his wetsuit, feeling along his collarbone to his shoulder. "What is it?" he said.

"I don't know. I feel funny, like this has happened before."

"A déja vu?"

"I don't know."

We danced close for a while with my face in his neck and hand on his collarbone. "Will Gabe be mad I took you away from him?" he asked.

"Gabe? Is Gabe here?"

"The lobster."

"Gabe is the Giant Lobster?"

"You didn't know?" he said. He lifted my shirttail and ran his fingers along the small of my back. "You seemed so sad. So I took you away."

I listened to the music, felt Getz's fingers against my back, and his pulse against my eyelids, and I tried to forget everything. But it all seemed so strangely familiar, the way he felt, as if I had dreamed it. I lifted my head.

"I feel dizzy," I said. "I have to sit down."

He left me on the bench with my head between my knees, and went to get me some water. I didn't feel bad actually, just loose, as if I might float apart. Getz said it was the lack of oxygen, like when a scuba diver gets too much nitrogen. Raptures of the Deep, he called it.

"Hey, babe," a man's voice said. "I never got a chance to thank you for delivering that statement." I looked to the side without lifting my head. Harper Martin sat down next to me on the bench. "I told you Dan Rather would grant you an audience. He's not the Pope you know."

I sat up. "Dan must be harder to see than the Pope by now," I said. "Thanks to you."

"I like your costume."

"Yours is more original. Imagine, if there's any Feds here looking for you they'll think you're the Giant Squid or the Empire State Building or something. No one would ever have foreseen that your best camouflage would be to come as yourself."

"I wanted to come as Liza Minnelli. But look, doll, we haven't got much time. I've got more messages for you to deliver. Will you be a sweetheart?" He pulled two envelopes out of the inside pocket of his leather jacket.

"Are there two?" I said. "I'm dizzy."

"This one is for the Maniac Drifter Inc. investors. They're having a secret meeting tomorrow at the Beachcombers. The second is for Dan Rather. Now don't get them confused. Dan's is a bio sheet. It would be completely useless to the investors."

I took the envelopes and tucked them in the inside pocket of my leather jacket.

"I like your style," he said. I nodded. "There's one hitch, babe. The Beachcombers Club is men only. You've gotta go in there dressed as a man—for the sake of decorum, you know?"

"What the hell," I said. I felt too strange to protest. I bent my head. When I looked up again Harper was gone, and Getz was standing over me with a glass of water in his hand. I had no idea when Harper had left or how much time had passed. I felt in my jacket pocket for the envelopes. They were there, so Harper had come after all. I had not dreamed it.

"Come on," Getz said. "They're closing up. We'll go to my house. There's lots of windows. "It'll be breezy there."

***

Tuesday

When I woke up Tuesday morning I found that I was in bed with Getz at his house and the television was on. Dan Rather was reporting the Temple of the Jaguars story update. He said the Federal Bureau of Investigation had delivered an official statement to the press, saying that they could not make amnesty for Harper's collaborators a condition of his surrender, and that the sooner he turned himself in the better the chances that the collaborators would not be prosecuted. Getz got out of bed. "Damn," he said. "No amnesty for the collaborators."

Dan Rather went on to say that a White House spokesman had criticized the extensive press coverage of this news item, saying the press had turned a simple U.S. Trade violation into a major media event, and had turned Harper Martin into an American Outlaw-Hero, as portrayed by Clint Eastwood in his movie roles. The White House spokesman had gone on to say that the news media was allowing Harper Martin to use their sympathies to manipulate public opinion in favor of the Nicaraguan government, and against the U.S.-backed Contra rebels.

"Is it night time?" I said. I was hoping I had just woken up from a nap after the Costume Ball and had not broken my promise to Gabe again.

Getz came in from the kitchen. "It's Tuesday morning. Do you have a hangover?"

"I wasn't drunk," I said. So I had broken my promise. "Dan Rather does the morning news now? I thought he only did the evening news."

"Dan Rather does all the Temple of the Jaguars reports. Day or night. How do you feel? You were really drunk last night."

"I didn't have anything to drink except club soda."

"What was the matter then?"

"I don't know."

On the television Dan Rather promised to provide coverage of Benefit Week in Provincetown and a profile of Harper Martin in upcoming reports, as well as updates on the government position. "There was a Harper Martin look-alike talking to you when I came back with your water. What did he say to you?" Getz asked. "He looked like a Fed."

"He was just a guy," I said. I reached over to the chair next to the bed, and felt inside my jacket for the envelopes. They were still there.

"What did he say to you? Did he ask you where Harper was?"

"I don't remember."

"How do you know they didn't drug you and then get information out of you about Harper?"

"Last night you told me I was a cop. This morning I'm the victim of a Federal drugging and illegal interrogation. I think you've seen too many cop movies."

"So you remember that part, when I told you you might be a cop."

"That was early in the evening. Something happened on the dance floor. I got dizzy. I started to feel strange. I don't remember much after that." It was true; I did not remember much, except Harper's visit, and the envelopes I had to deliver.

"So they drugged your club soda and made you tell them where Harper is."

"I think you've seen too many cop movies," I repeated.

"You're the one whose mother worked for the FBI."

"Who told you that?"

He looked at me incredulously. "You don't remember? It was the middle of the night. You were sober by then."

I sat up on the edge of the bed, threw my legs over and chuckled to myself. I could not believe the situations my amnesia got me into—I could not believe I did not know what had happened that night Joe and Gabe kept referring to, I did not know where my clothes had been when I woke up that morning at Gabe's, I did not know who had left the note on my pillow about lighting a cigarette on my thigh. And now I had broken my promise again.

"Getz, can I ask you something?"

"Sure."

"How come we haven't seen each other in a couple weeks?"

"We see each other all the time."

"You know what I mean. It's been two weeks since I stayed here."

"You don't remember why?"

I shook my head guiltily. Remember. Remember. What a word.

"You said you'd come back the next night and you never did."

"I said I'd come back?"

"Don't you remember? You took Gabe home. I ended up with Blaine. Then I got busy lobstering. I don't know. Who knows? Does anybody know why people end up together or with somebody else? Now you're here and Blaine went home with Dominic. I don't know. I don't know anything."

"Blaine went home with Dominic last night?" I asked.

"Yeah, don't you remember?"

"No, it must have been late, when I was dizzy."

"Can I ask you a question?"

"Sure."

"Are you in Alcoholics Anonymous?" I shook my head. "Are you on the wagon?"

"No, why?"

"Because you never drink, and you eat a lot of sweets. The people I know in AA crave sweets. And then you can't remember things in the morning, like a drunk who got so plastered the night before he can't remember the fights he got into or the insults he handed out."

A drunk person's amnesia. That was what I had. I had never thought of it in those terms before. "But why do you think I crave sweets?" I said.

"You're always drinking chocolate egg creams and eating Hershey Bars."

"That's chocolate, not sugar," I said. I got out of bed and gave him a consoling pat on my way to the shower. He did not believe a word of it.

***

I took a commuter flight down to New York City, provided Harper's biographical information packet to Dan Rather at the CBS News offices and was back in Provincetown in time to deliver Harper's letter to the secret investors' meeting. I was getting to be a pro at this espionage work. I thought perhaps I should become a private investigator, or take after my mother and work for the FBI.

Then I went to the secret investor's meeting at the Beachcombers disguised as Harper Martin. The big wooden door to the Hulk was unlocked; I swung it open and stepped inside. No one was in the front room. I walked around a ping-pong table with florescent lights strung up above it. A ping-pong paddle lay on either end of the table, as if someone had just stopped playing. I passed between the table and stacks of shingles, piles of beer bottles, stools and ladders, to a mantle at the far end of the room, which was decorated with whale vertebrae and a model of a schooner. Above the mantle hung a framed news clipping of Charles Heinz in his studio, "shortly before his death," the caption said. I inspected an old poster for the Annual Beachcombers Ball, which was titled "Clown Prince, Prisoner of Paris." Beneath that a chalkboard chart titled "Proposed Members List," with lines and columns for votes, recommendations and commentary, leaned against the wall. The Beachcombers decided on members by first rejecting the candidate by unanimously shouting *No!* when the vote was called. Then the Skipper announced the candidate had been unanimously elected.

The Beachcombers met in a big wooden barn-like structure called "The Hulk." It was located on the east end of town, on the water side, across the street from the Art Association. The Beachcombers bought the Hulk in 1917 for $2000. At that time it jutted out into the bay on a wharf, but in 1927 a big storm weakened the main wharf pilings and they had to turn the Hulk around sideways.

The Beachcombers began as a club for men who were "engaged in the practice of fine arts or their branches." In the fifties, when the Abstract Expressionists became a force in town, Hawthorne and the Beachcombers came to be known as the more conservative group, the craftsmen-artists. Now the sons of these artists were the Beachcombers. They still met in the Hulk to have dinner together, get drunk, tell stories and piss off the deck, play pool and sleep in the wall bunks.

The Hulk looked almost the same now in the 1980s as it had when the Beachcombers bought it 70 years before, except it had been turned around sideways, and the posters for the shows and annual balls, the photographs and documents, had accumulated the weight of memory and history. Now, when a person walked in the Beachcombers, he couldn't help feeling that this was an important place, where history was made, where famous artists like Hawthorne, Ambrose Webster, and Edwin Dickinson had gathered. Where the artwork and photographs, junk and memorabilia had once seemed offhand, careless even, they now seemed precious and revealing, a testament to the famous people who had belonged there, like the studio where Picasso painted the *Guernica* or the desk where Dickens wrote *Great Expectations*.

I looked out the back window at the deck and the bay. I could hear Cosmo and Raphael talking upstairs, but I didn't go up just yet. There was another room downstairs and I wanted to look at it first. I went through the door, stood underneath the fireplace and read the signatures carved in the bricks inlaid along the mantle. I ran my hand along the wide wooden captain's table that was set with tin plates and mugs for 12 people. At the head of the table was a wood gavel laid out above the plate, carved in the shape of a penis with testicles. I grabbed the head of the penis and rapped the testicles on the table. "Order! Order!" I shouted. Along the wall that looked out on the deck and bay were two long tables with pots and pans spread out to dry. A poker table sat in the corner of the room, and on it a circular rack with colored chips stacked in the runners. Photos of old guys with beards and sailor caps were nailed to the beams and pots and lanterns hung from hooks in the ceiling.

When Cosmo came into the kitchen, I was reading a poem by Harry Kemp, the dune poet, that was framed and hanging on the wall. "Was that you shouting?" he said.

"I was trying out the gavel," I said.

"How about this?" he said. He walked behind me to the corner of the room and plugged an electric cord into the socket underneath the window. A sculpture of a naked woman with electric light bulbs for nipples flashed above his head. They were blinking on and off like a Christmas Tree.

"Charmed," I said.

"Here for the meeting?" he said.

I nodded. "I have a message from Harper." I reached into my jacket and pulled out the envelope. "Can I bring it up?" He motioned for me to follow him, and when he got to the stairs stepped back to let me pass. "After you," I said.

"Ladies first," he said. I grimaced and went up. "So is Nichole coming to the Bocce Tournament tomorrow?" he asked as we passed a ceramic flounder hanging from a shingle along the stairwell.

“How did you know it was me?” I said. He laughed. “Harper told me to come dressed as a man.”

“Well you did that. Is she coming?”

“I don’t know.”

“Maybe you should talk to her.”

I stopped on the stairs and turned around. “I’ll try.”

The upstairs room was dominated by an enormous wooden pool table with leather ball pouches. Old car seats were rigged up along the walls as spectator benches. “This way,” Cosmo said. I followed him into a back room, which also had a pool table in it. The investors of Maniac Drifter Inc. were using it as a conference table, and had their notebooks, papers and pens strewn across the green felt. Antaeus held the black eight ball in his hand, then spun it across the table so it ricocheted near the middle pocket where Falzano was sitting, bounced off the far end where Cosmo had left his chair empty, and came to rest between him and Raphael.

I looked around. Above the deck windows hung framed etchings of George Washington and Abraham Lincoln. A flood lamp from the submarine S-4 sunk off Wood End on December 17, 1927, was mounted in a class case on the wall behind me. A crumpled Winston pack sat on the floor by Antaeus’ feet, and an old Louis XIV chair with ripped upholstery was stationed by a tiny room. I walked over to inspect it. It was the john. “Nobody uses that,” Antaeus said. “They piss off the deck.”

“I don’t,” Falzano said.

“You don’t come here,” Antaeus said.

“The hell she doesn’t,” Raphael said.

Antaeus spun the eight ball across the table again, but

Falzano had pushed her notebook out and it interfered with his rebound. "Damn," he said, and walked around the table to retrieve the ball. "So you caught a spy?" he said to Cosmo.

Cosmo patted me on the back. I pulled my fedora down lower on my forehead. Antaeus thought it was a greeting and nodded back to me. "A messenger," Cosmo said. "He brought a letter from Harper." Raphael pulled up the Louis XIV chair and invited me to sit down. I smiled at him, tucked some stuffing back into the chair, sat down, and placed the letter on the pool table in front of Cosmo.

"Should he stay?" Antaeus said, looking curiously at me.

"I think it's alright," Cosmo said. "I know him."

Raphael smiled. Falzano cocked her head like a dog who has heard the word "cat" or "bird." "I think I know him, too," she said.

Cosmo slipped the letter out of the envelope and unfolded it. "To the investors of Maniac Drifter Inc.," he read aloud, in his formal, stentorian voice, the one he reserved for speeches at the Art Association. "I wanted to let you know that I am turning myself in to the Federal Government representatives tomorrow, in answer to their subpoena for questioning on U.S. Trade and Customs Violations." Cosmo looked up over the page to see how the others reacted. Antaeus slumped in his chair and twirled the eight ball on the table with his fingertips, staring down at it as if he were a young boy who had just been scolded. Falzano looked around the room, tapping her pen on her notebook. Raphael fixed his eyes on Cosmo and the letter.

"And then?" Raphael said.

Cosmo cleared his throat. "Then it says: I plan to invoke the secrecy clause, Article Eight of Maniac Drifter's

Articles of Incorporation. If you remember, that clause states that you granted me complete privacy as to the corporation's activities and understand that those activities are within the law. This article will serve as a *signed statement*, (emphasis Harper's), that you were not aware of any illegal activities, and would not condone them had you been aware." Cosmo looked up from the page again.

"Hogwash," Falzano said. She was drumming on her notebook with the pen now. "Just because you don't know something illegal is going on doesn't mean you're not responsible. If they want to subpoena us they will."

"Holy Mother of God," Antaeus said, as if he just remembered something.

"We've all been investigated for something at one time or another," Cosmo said, looking over at Antaeus.

"Think of the press he's getting," Raphael said. "It's working against the government. They're under pressure. They'll just want to get rid of this thing."

"Shall I continue?" Cosmo said. Antaeus looked up. Falzano nodded her head. "I know this is not legally binding, but I've been in touch with some of the Federal government representatives, and I'm pretty sure by this time, with all the publicity, they'll be willing to settle with me as simply as possible. I hope to be out again by the end of the week, and I believe that even after the trade and customs violations fines, taxes and interest fees, I'll be able to meet my monthly payment." Cosmo looked up again, like a schoolteacher expecting a response.

"The smart ass," Antaeus said, laughing. "He's probably into six figures by now, and he's reassuring us about his monthly payment."

"It sounds like he knows what's going to happen before he even turns himself in," Falzano said.

"They must have made a deal," Antaeus said. "The Feds do that, you know."

"The boy isn't stupid," Raphael said. "We all knew he had a business sense."

"Is that it?" Falzano asked Cosmo.

Cosmo returned to the letter. "He finishes with: The Defense Fund and Benefit Week were great ideas. Thanks for your backing. See you soon." Cosmo folded the letter and put it back into its envelope.

"So what do you think?" Falzano asked, to no one in particular.

"I think Harper Martin is the best investment we ever made," Cosmo said gravely.

Antaeus started laughing as if he suddenly understood the joke. "We're going to be rich!" he said. "The whole town is going to be rich!" Raphael smiled contentedly, as if he had reached some cosmic understanding about the universe. "The smart-ass bastard," Antaeus said.

"Should we publicize this secrecy clause as a way to garner public opinion and discourage the feds from indicting us?" Falzano said.

"I don't think we need to," Cosmo said. "But I think he wants us to go on with Benefit Week, if I'm reading the letter right." He patted the envelope with his fingertips. "Even if he won't need the Defense Fund money."

"I think that's exactly right," Raphael said, growing more and more Buddha-like as some color rose to his cheeks.

"The son of a bitch," Antaeus said, slamming his fist down on the table. "He's going to look like he made this big sacrifice, turning himself in, taking the rap on himself. He's made himself into a goddamn hero!"

"Precisely," Raphael said, getting up.

"The best investment this town ever made," Cosmo repeated. "Nobody loses."

"For a change," Antaeus said.

The investors of Maniac Drifter Inc. gathered up their papers and notebooks. Antaeus rolled the eight ball into the side pocket near Falzano. Raphael held my chair for me as I got up, and then took me by the elbow with his hand. "Let me see you out," he said, nodding toward the door.

"Well, thank you for bringing this, young man," Cosmo said to me.

I nodded. "He didn't say a word the whole time," Falzano whispered as I walked downstairs with Raphael.

When we reached the door of the Hulk, Raphael squeezed my arm and said, "Mary's back from Boston. I thought you might like to know." He winked at me.

"How did you know it was me?" I said.

"Mary was over at the house last night talking to Elaine," Raphael said. "They mentioned that you worked for Ruth Allen, at the law office. I thought you must be the girl present at the investors' meeting there, so naturally, when I saw you today I made the connection."

"They were talking about me?" I said.

"I think she'd like to see you," Raphael said. "Will you be at Paradiso's benefit Thursday night?" I said I would. "Mary will be working then."

"Thanks," I said.

"Good luck," Raphael said, and went back upstairs, his smile exuding the mystical aura he had just acquired.

***

At Cosmo's restaurant, the front dining room had windows on Commercial Street. You had to pass through the kitchen to get to the rear dining room, which extended out on stilts to the bay, and had windows on the water, facing the coast guard wharf. The walls in the front dining room were cluttered with old photographs of Provincetown and Italy, faded posters for gallery exhibits and shows at the Provincetown Playhouse, wine bottles, boat buoys, pulleys and fishing nets. Some of Cosmo's seascapes hung in the rear dining room. In both rooms the rafters held up oars, poles, boat masts and sails, rolls of tarp and canvas, and old picture frames.

When I arrived at the restaurant that night it was booked solid from the first seatings at six until ten, so Gabe had set up the television in the kitchen, where the waiters and waitresses could catch glimpses of the *CBS Evening News* Temple of the Jaguars Report when they dropped off their orders or picked up their food.

I listened to the report while I made salads, constructed antipasto plates and filled cannoli. That evening's report was on the contents of the crates that had been confiscated by the FBI. With all the activities, I had not had a chance to find out much on my own about the skin-suit man, or even to take him out of his hiding place and run my hands over his double skin, so I was anxious to hear the report.

Blaine walked into the kitchen clutching menus against her chest, and stood transfixed in front of the television. "Would you look at that," she said, pointing to the screen. "Dominic, Gabe, Kate, it's a jade mask. Isn't that jade? Look how smooth."

Dominic glanced up from the oven where he was bringing out a pan of cannelloni. He saw the mask and nodded. Gabe leaned back away from the kettle of pasta, and looked at the screen. Then he shook his head and gave out a little one-breath laugh. "It figures," he said, "that a woman who likes fast cars and minks would like a jade mask, even if it is for the deceased. You put that mask on your mummied uncle, dear. That's what it's for."

Blaine sighed and gave him a disdainful, superior look, as if he were not capable of appreciating great art. She wandered around the aluminum refrigerator to my side of the kitchen and whispered: "Isn't it beautiful?"

By this time customers had crowded in the doorway, so Blaine rushed from the kitchen to seat them. Gabe chuckled to himself while he stirred the pasta, as if he were relishing some private insight. Dominic placed a tray of lasagna into the oven. Then he came over to where I was busy at the prep counter, stood behind me, and watched me arrange an antipasto plate. "Have I ever told you how much the customers admire your antipasto plates?" Dominic said, throwing the towel over his shoulder.

"Admire?" Gabe said. "They're supposed to eat them."

"Antaeus once said they were architectonic," Dominic said, patting me on the shoulder.

"Don't give her any encouragement," Gabe said. "She's vain enough already."

"Are you two fighting again?" Dominic said.

"Fighting!" Gabe said. He picked up the kettle and poured the steaming water out into the sink, so only the pasta was left. "Fighting! We're not even talking! We don't see each other anymore."

"You saw each other this afternoon at the windsurfing regatta," Dominic said. "You saw each other last night at the White Sands Costume Ball."

"And nothing in between," Gabe said. "My point exactly."

"Looks like you're in trouble, girl," Dominic said.

"But what about you, Dom?" Gabe said. "Still with Blaine?" He winked at Dominic.

"How did you know about that?" Dominic said. I started laughing.

"So are you still together?" Gabe said.

"What do you mean 'still'?" Dominic said. "We've only been together since last night."

"That's about as long as it lasts," Gabe said. He started a new kettle to boil. He had a serene, self-satisfied look on his face, as if he had just retaliated for the only two things that were bothering him.

"I thought only Aztecs did that," Dominic said, pointing to the television.

"Did what?" Gabe said.

"Ritual sacrifice. This temple's supposed to be Mayan."

"The Toltec Mayans practiced it," Gabe said.

"How do you know?" I said.

"We studied Pre-Columbian Art at Pratt," Gabe said.

"I always forget you used to be a graphic designer," I said.

"Don't feel bad," Dominic said. "Everyone forgets."

"Good," Gabe said.

I had finished making all the salads and cannoli the waiters needed for the time being, so I went out to the front dining room to look at the customers. Tuesday was usually a slow night at the restaurant. Not many people came in, and those who did were usually locals or summer residents, who had that night off after the hectic weekend. But tonight, after a week of *CBS News* Temple of the Jaguar Reports, temple updates, and news reports about the Harper Martin Defense Fund and Benefit Week in Provincetown, the restaurant was packed with summer residents from up-Cape, tourists from Boston, Providence and New York, people who should have gone home Sunday night. Some of them had taken a week's vacation at the spur of the moment, just to attend the Benefit Week. They carried lists of the Benefit activities along with their maps and ferry schedules, and were trying to decide which events to go see. They talked about the celebrities they might run into in town, and looked around at the other tables in case a famous painter, writer, or television news anchorman might be in the restaurant at that very moment.

Lance rushed into the kitchen, tore off the order sheet from his pad, clipped it on the metal wheel hanging in the kitchen, and spun it around to face Gabe and Dominic. "One parm, one carbonara, a stuffed flounder and a shrimp adriatico." He went back around to the doorway of the dining room where I was still standing. "Four salads please, dear," he said, bowing.

While I prepared the salads, I listened to Dan Rather describe the contents of another confiscated crate. I was hoping he would get to the one I had opened, and explain what the CBS researchers and Carnegie Institute archaeologists knew about the two-faced woman, the whistling couple, the skeleton man, and especially the skin-suit man. But Dan was showing slides of the laughing figurines from the Nicaraguan Lake District.

Dominic yelled to Lance that his order was up. Lance

hurried in, arranged the plates on a serving tray, and swung the tray up over his shoulder. I worked on the desserts now. Cosmo came over from the hostess station and watched me garnish a ricotta pie. "So what's with Nichole?" he asked. "Have you seen her?" She had not shown up at the windsurf races, and Cosmo had hoped she would, since he sponsored them at the restaurant.

"She spends a lot of time working on the house," I said. I set the pie on the counter. "You'll find her over there."

Cosmo seemed to be absorbed in watching The Temple of the Jaguars Report, but added: "That Frank is probably there."

"Nichole is helping Frank work on the house," I said. Cosmo made it sound as if Frank were over there sunbathing and drinking ice tea.

"He's an opportunist," he said.

Dominic walked over to the refrigerator and caught my wrist as he went by. When I looked at him, he shook his head. "He works hard," I said. "Harder than any of us. So does Nichole."

"Well I guess she's paying him for it," Cosmo said. "And he's ruining her life. But she won't listen—not to me. Not to her own father. I've brought people into this town ... Dominic ... Getz. I've made lives for them. But my own daughter quits me and won't listen to me. She won't learn. Except the hard way."

Dominic had grabbed my arm and was shaking his head vehemently. "You wanted something once," I said quietly.

"That's exactly right," Cosmo said, turning away from the television to look at me, as if someone jarred him awake.

"I wanted something once. But I bit the bullet. I stayed with my wife, I kept the family together, I kept the restaurant afloat, so Nichole and Dominic and people like them, young people, would have something. And then she does this to me."

Cosmo had owned a restaurant with Nello once, when they were friends, fellow painters and business partners. The restaurant was called Nello's and it was located on the east end of town near the Beachcombers and Art Association. The story was that Cosmo was having an affair with Nello's wife and Nello found out. Nello's wife left town and Cosmo started his own restaurant on the west end. Nello remarried and kept the east end restaurant. It seemed as if Nello's wife got the bad deal, run out of town like that. Some people thought Cosmo's wife had it the worst, publically embarrassed. Nichole thought that she, as Cosmo's daughter, had suffered the most. The true romantics thought Cosmo had it the worst, because he really loved Nello's wife and now he had to live without her, and had to stay in town with the mess he'd made, knowing he'd betrayed his wife and his best friend.

"It's not like Nichole did it to spite you," I said. "She fell in love with someone."

Cosmo took the knife out of Dominic's hands and began shelling prawns. "So did I," he said. He pointed the knife at me. "So did I."

Dominic took my hand and said he needed something from the Land Ho. "You can help me carry." I nodded dumbly and followed him. Gabe winked at me through the steam from the pasta kettles, and Blaine glared at me when we passed the hostess station. When we were inside the Land Ho, Dominic sat me down at the table. "I understand what

you're trying to do," he said. "But keep in mind that nobody ever talks to Cosmo that way—not his wife, not me, not even the Selectmen. He's one of the people who run this town."
"So why did he let me? Because I'm an outsider? Because I don't know any better?"

Dominic shook his head. "Because you're Nichole's friend. He must feel pretty bad. I've never seen him expose himself like that. Not in 20 years. He wants his daughter back, Kate."

"On his own terms," I said. "And he wants me to help him. I'm no hero, Dom; and Nichole really loves this guy. I can't tell her what to do. Not that she'd listen."

"You can try."

"Okay," I said. "Okay."

When we returned to the kitchen, Cosmo was at the hostess station, talking to Blaine. Blaine was on the inside of the station, where the cashier usually sat. She leaned her elbows on the counter and looked up at Cosmo, who was also leaning over, from the outside, so they looked as if they were gossiping or confiding in each other. Blaine made a pout with her lips, then rubbed Cosmo's arm with her hand, and tugged at the end of his goatee.

After Cosmo left her to visit the dining rooms, Blaine came into the kitchen and watched me carefully, as if she wanted to learn how to make the desserts herself. Then she turned around to watch the television. "I heard you and Nichole are going to judge the Bocce Tournament tomorrow," she said.

"I'm not sure Nichole's coming," I said. I put two spumonis and a chocolate mousse on the high counter to be picked up.

"Why wouldn't she come?" she said, her voice arcing up into an innocent, youthful whine. She kept her eyes on the television.

"She just might not come, that's all."

Blaine was staring at the television without really looking at it, the way infants watch the shapes and colors in a mobile. She turned back to me, leaning her elbows conspiratorially on the prep counter. "Maybe you could talk to her," she said. "I know it would mean a lot to Cosmo."

I shrugged and shook my head. "He knows where she lives, you know," I said.

"But Frank's over at the house," she whispered, leaning over a wedge of ricotta pie.

"So what?" I said.

"Please talk to her, please."

"I'll try. I just don't see why Cosmo can't go over to her house himself if he wants to talk to her."

Blaine stood up and folded her arms across her chest. "Cosmo's done a lot for this town," she said. "You probably weren't here when it started so you don't remember. He took Dominic in after his dad died, and he brought Getz out here from Rhode Island, and he ran the Art Association. And he's been through a lot, too. You weren't here for that either. You just don't understand." She burst into tears and rushed through the kitchen toward the rear dining room, where the restrooms were located.

Now Dan Rather was showing a picture of the skin-suit man. Dan said it was a representation of the cult god Xipe Totec. Dan explained that Xipe Totec was worshipped in the spring. He was the god of fertility, he protected the harvest, and the planting. To invoke the god, a young man was celebrated all year as the god's representative, and then in the spring the young man was sacrificed and flayed, and his skin was worn by another member of the village. This was supposed to signify replanting, the symbol of the live seed in the dead husk.

The god was believed to manifest itself in the man who wore the young man's flayed skin. And this man, by wearing the skin of the other man, was believed to take on godly attributes. During the festival of the gods, this man in the flayed skin walked among the villagers and became a living cult image. So the stone statues and replicas of the god Xipe Totec were not images of a god, but of a man wearing another man's skin, to invoke the god and make it manifest in him. So it was really a statue of a god impersonator.

Dan Rather was explaining that the figure on the screen was cut out of lava stone. The man was sitting cross-legged, as the viewers could see, with his wrists resting on his knees. The mask he was wearing was the skin of the flayed young man, tied at the back of the head in elaborate knots like those carved on the caryatids of Tula. The jumpsuit he was wearing was again the skin of the flayed young man, with bows at the shoulders and waist. The rest of the skin appeared to be intact, Dan said, except for the flayed man's hands, which dangled from the wearer's hands, and the stitching around an incision on the chest, where the heart had been removed.

"I guess the Frank Sinatra song, 'I've Got You Under My Skin' takes on new meaning after you see this program," Lance said.

I remembered how delighted I had been when I found

the crates at Hatches Harbor, since I thought Harper had shipped them all away. I remembered all the dragonflies buzzing and the seagulls crowded around the place. I remembered how carefully I had pried open the crate; it seemed like it took hours. And then I had brushed the straw back very carefully, and lifted each figure out, examined it, and put it back again in the exact same place in the straw —except for the skin-suit man. I had kept him, for good luck maybe—maybe for a wish.

Gabe finished making pasta marinara and came over to the television. He put his arm around my shoulder. "We studied this," he said. He pointed to the screen. "I could probably tell you more about it, if you're interested." He waved his finger around at the screen.

"Really?" I said. I looked at him as if he were someone I had never met before.

"This is just an overview. You know, for a television audience." He kissed my forehead and went back to work.

Dan Rather was saying that these people believed that certain clothing symbolized a transformation of the real through magic, and that magic could be compelled through the change of appearances. Dan said they believed that, in rituals involving certain skirt forms, hairstyles, jewelry and face paint, they could invoke the gods and compel them to manifest themselves, temporarily, inside the human being wearing the special costume.

At ten o'clock, I cleaned the prep station, secured plastic wrap over the bowl of cannoli filling, threw the serving knives in the dirty dishes pile and took my apron off. Gabe approached me. "Going to Paradiso's?" he said.

"I think I'm going home," I said.

"Would you rather wait upstairs? At my place?" He put his arm around me.

"I think I want to go home."

"Well, why don't you wait thirty minutes, and I'll go with you?"

"I think I want to be alone."

"Alone!" he said. "You're never alone. You weren't alone last night."

I thought back to the White Sands Costume Ball the night before, and watching the Temple of the Jaguar report that morning from Getz's bed. Of course, I could not remember anything in between, so I had to assume I had been with Getz.

"Kate," Gabe was saying. "Kate." I looked up at him. "Remember how you answered my questions a couple weeks ago? Remember your promise?"

I hoped he was referring to the question he had posed in the daytime, the one I could remember. Gabe had asked me if I would not sleep with anyone but him. "I promised I'd *try*," I said.

"You're not trying very hard."

"Look, you can walk me home if that'll make you feel better, but I really want to be alone tonight."

"Walk you home! I've made that mistake once before. No thank you."

I looked at him, puzzled. Was that the Sunday night with Joe that everyone was always talking about?

"So don't stand there looking coy," he said. "Go home."

I turned and went.

***

Wednesday

When I woke up Wednesday morning, I found that I was home, and in bed with Harper Martin. He was sitting propped up on the pillows, naked except for his fedora and string tie, reading *The Maltese Falcon*. When he saw that I was awake, he winked at me. "Hi, doll," he said. "How was your beauty rest?"

"Harper Martin!" I said, jumped out of bed, and then, finding I did not have any clothes on, climbed back in again. "Harper Martin! What are you doing here?"

"It's like I told you last night, babe," he said, setting the book down on the nightstand. "I'm like a man sentenced to death. Every man gets his last wish. So you granted it to me, don't you remember?"

I looked at him astonished and tried with all my might to remember, but I couldn't.

"It's like a man on his way to the electric chair, and before he goes in, they ask him if he wants to make a phone call, or say a prayer or make a statement, but he asks the jailer for a cigarette. A cigarette. It's like that. You're like that. Like a cigarette."

Harper leaned over and took the pack of Marlboros off the nightstand. He extracted a cigarette from the pack, tamped it on his knuckles, ripped off the filter, and placed the cigarette between his lips.

"By the way," he said, "you gotta light?"

I pointed to the nightstand, where a matchbook was lying next to his cigarette pack. Harper touched the rim of his fedora, took up the matches and lit his cigarette. He leaned back on the pillows, and let the smoke out languorously. Then he looked at me again, tousled my hair with his free hand and put his fedora on my head.

"So how's my girl this morning? Did you get your beauty rest? You were pretty mad when I snuck in so late and woke you up."

I was still staring at him. I was wondering if I had ever slept with him before. I was wondering if he was the one who had left the note on my pillow that said, *You're so hot I could light a cigarette on your thigh.* But to find that out I would have to confess my amnesia, and I didn't want to. I was especially wondering if he had already been given a jail term, since he kept talking about himself as a man sentenced to death. But that could not have happened overnight. Didn't he have to go to trial first? After all, this was America. He hadn't even turned himself in for questioning yet.

Harper took his watch off the nightstand and fastened it around his wrist. Judging from the nightstand it seemed as if he could have been in bed for several days. A bottle of Jack Daniels and two glasses with melted ice in them, an ashtray full of Marlboros with the filters ripped off, and several scraps of folded paper lay on the table. One of the papers had phone numbers written on it, another calculations. Harper's wallet also lay on open on the nightstand with its credit cards and dollar bills spilling out. Next to that was a set of keys, two plastic pens, a rubber band, a plastic comb and three toothpicks.

Harper climbed out of bed and walked over to the dresser. He patted a television set that was sitting on top of it. "See what I brought you?" Then he leaned over and plugged it in. I thought he was very nice looking with his clothes off. I did not remember ever seeing him that way before. I hoped we would not make love again so I would be able to remember. That would be something. But why was he wearing his tie?

Harper switched the television on. "See what I brought you?" he repeated. When the picture came clear, he turned the dial to Channel Two and got back into bed again. "I thought that since I was turning myself in to the Feds, from now on you'd want to be able to watch the CBS News and the Temple of the Jaguar Reports at home." He put his arm around me, pulled me gently against him and kissed me.

"You're turning yourself in this morning?" I said.

"Of course. Isn't that what last night was all about?"

"I delivered one letter to the investors' meeting and the other to Dan Rather."

"I know. You were brilliant. But you're missing the update. Watch." He pointed to the screen.

I looked at a shot of Provincetown, somewhere on Bradford Street, early in the morning. The TV camera scanned the street, where a crowd of people was lined up behind a barricade, and the neighbors were leaning out their windows or sitting on their porches. In front of a three-story white house, a crowd of reporters had congregated with their cameras on their shoulders, microphones in their hands and cables trailing behind them to their vans. The television showed a closer view of the house, focusing in on the front door, then the windows on each floor going up to the third story, then the two skylights on the sloped roof.

"That's this house!" I screamed.

"That's right now," he said.

The TV commentator said that the crowd was anxious for the Federal Marshals to arrive, and for Harper to appear. They hoped he would make a statement.

"Jesus Christ!" I said, jumping out of bed and looking around frantically for my clothes. "Is the door locked? Are they coming up now? Are the reporters coming?"

"Relax. I locked the door. Nobody's coming. And nobody will see you if you stop running back and forth in front of the windows. They're shooting this live, you know."

"Shooting!" I said, diving into bed with an improvised set of clothes on. I zippered, snapped and buttoned, pulled my socks up, tied the laces of my sneakers, brushed my hair and pulled the covers up. "Am I going to get arrested?"

"Who would arrest you? Don't be silly." He put out his cigarette and took his fedora from my head. "The Feds aren't coming until nine," he said. "Can I use your shower?" I nodded. "Will you make some French toast? I said yes. "That's my girl."

He put on his white shirt and flicked the tie underneath the collar. He pulled on his jockey shorts, chinos, socks, and stuffed his wallet, wads of paper, pens, and keys into his pockets. Leaving his jacket off, he went into the bathroom, turned on the shower water and burst out singing, *You must remember this, a kiss is just a kiss—*

When he emerged from the bathroom, fully dressed except for his wing tips and leather jacket, I had the French toast ready. He carried the TV into the kitchen and positioned it on the day bed. Harper put on his shoes and sat down at the kitchen table.

"You always have the best syrup," he said, pouring a generous portion onto his French toast.

It was ten minutes to nine. I turned the television sound off, so I could hear what was going on in the street. It was too confusing to listen to the same sounds on the TV that I could hear out the windows. When Harper was finished eating, he got up and began to wash the dishes.

"I'll do that," I said.

"Wouldn't think of it."

I remained at the table, watching the TV and listening to the noises outside. I could hear the generalized hum of people talking to each other, and above that people shouting messages to Harper.

I watched Harper finish the dishes. He was humming "I Get a Kick Out of You" and had an aura of domestic harmony about him, as if he had been living with me for years, and this was a normal day, like any other one, when nothing out of the ordinary was going to happen. Then I began to hear another noise—a low ominous drone, like the dragonflies at Long Point Light, only stronger, and more sinister. The floor and windows began to shake.

"It's an earthquake!" I said and ran for the door. Then I remembered the reporters downstairs and ran back again.

"It's not an earthquake. You lived in Los Angeles too long. It's my ride." He dried his hands, draped the towel over the sink, and pointed up at the roof.

"A helicopter?" I said, looking up at the ceiling and then at the television. I went to the skylight and tried to see out without showing myself.

"An army helicopter," he said, pointing to the TV. "Double rotors."

"Why didn't you tell them to pick you up on the ground?" I said. I knew this had been his idea. He was showing off again, making everything larger than life, like the movies.

"I have this fear of the ground," he said, putting his leather jacket on and adjusting his fedora and string tie. "And anyway, the Feds asked me to avoid the reporters."

He took me by the shoulders and kissed me once on each cheek, like a Frenchman. Then he gave me a bear hug and patted me vigorously on the back, like a Soviet President in a gargantuan fur coat might do on the national news. Then he bowed. Harper was getting ready for a public appearance, for interviews, government meetings and press conferences.

"Now be good," he said.

He cranked the skylight open, then hoisted himself up so he was sitting on the rim. The crowd cheered. He waved to them and blew them kisses. One of the helicopter pilots, in military fatigues, a helmet and headphones, offered Harper his hand to help him out onto the roof, but Harper shook his head and indicated that he would do it himself. The helicopter must have descended in order to pick him up, and it was roaring now. Harper shouted at me: "Remember what we talked about!" He blew me a kiss, climbed around the dome of the skylight, stood up on the sloped roof, and fell into the open arms of the helicopter man.

I crept over to the skylight and peered out, keeping my head down so I would not be seen. Harper and the helicopter man climbed up a short ladder into the machine, and it started to lift up again. When it was high enough, the house stopped shuddering and I could hear the crowd below shouting: "Free Harper Martin!" They were pointing at the helicopter and the skylight. I kept my eye on them, wondering if they were angry or excited, or simply curious. I thought about Harper's parting words: *Remember what we talked about*. I couldn't remember anything. But if I failed to, I would let him down. Whatever he had asked me to do, I wouldn't know what it was.

Now the crowd was shouting: "Free Harper Martin! Free the Temple of the Jaguars!" The camera crews still ran around in the street, some filming the crowd, some filming their newscasters, who pointed to the house, the skylight, and the spot in the sky where the helicopter had disappeared. I watched the whole thing on television.

Eventually the crowd thinned, the policemen took the barricades down and drove away. The reporters and cameramen began to come into the house, slowly, in twos and threes, and some of the people who had been watching followed them. I rushed to the door and made sure it was locked, then I pushed the kitchen table against it and stacked the chairs on top of that. Then I dove into the bed with all my clothes on and pulled the covers up over my head.

From my position under the covers, I could hear people walking up and down the stairs, knocking on doors, conferring with each other and with my neighbors. I could hear the camera crews shouting directions. At intervals people would knock on my door, but none of the chairs stacked against the kitchen table fell down. They would shout: "Excuse me!" through the door, and identify themselves and the call letters of their television stations. After that some of my neighbors tried knocking, even my landlord, but I stayed under the covers and eventually everyone gave up and went away. When it had been quiet for a while, I began to think about Harper again, and what he had said to me just before he climbed out of the skylight. *Remember what we talked about.* Again, I wondered what we had talked about, what I was supposed to do.

I pulled the covers off and sat up in bed. I reached over to the cupboard built into the wall, and slid the door open. Inside were a number of boxes I used for storage, where I kept old clothes, photographs, magazine articles, keepsakes and memorabilia, appliances that needed repair, items I no longer used, but did not have the heart to give away. In one of these boxes, underneath a broken alarm clock, a tea kettle, and a stuffed bear, I had hidden the skin-suit man. I pulled everything out of the box now, until I reached the bottom. The package was still there, wrapped up in an old sweater. I took the bundle out and unwrapped it.

I sat the skin-suit man on my lap and ran my fingers over him. I traced the outlines of the elaborate knot securing his mask, and the bows fastening the skin suit on him. I placed my fingertips in the palms of his real hands, and then in the palms of the hands dangling from the skin suit. I traced the edge of the mask underneath his chin, and the top of the suit, just below, around his neck and shoulders. I put my hand in his real mouth, then traced its outline, and then the outline of the mouth surrounding it, the one that belonged to the mask. The mouths were both slightly open. It made him look plaintive, as if he were longing for something, and was about to cry out. I put my finger through the eye of the mask, and tried to touch the real eyes down below, but the gap was deep and the eye slits narrow, so I could not reach through. I looked inside carefully, trying to locate the eyes, but they had not been carved in. I ran my fingertips along his arms and back, as if to smooth the skin suit down. The lava was porous, and made him look pockmarked, or scarred. I touched the stitches on the chest where the flayed man's heart had been removed.

I had guessed right about the skin-suit man—he was wearing another man's skin. The idea made me uneasy. I had seen men on the wharf flay fish, and even that turned my stomach. But the idea of a man actually wearing another man's skin, his legs inside the other man's legs, his arms inside the other man's arms, his chest against the other man's chest, his face peering out from beneath the other man's face—it unsettled me. *And this is how he gained his magic*, I thought. *This is how he let the god inside him.*

Chapter Three

When I was sure no reporters or curiosity seekers were still waiting downstairs, I went out. I intended to stop at Nichole's house on my way to the Bocce tournament.

Nichole had inherited the house on Miller Hill from her maternal grandmother. Her father Cosmo said she did not appreciate the house but she did. Acquiring property was the most amazing thing that had ever happened to her. It changed her life by bringing her back to Provincetown when she had vowed never to come back. It made her a landlord; she had also inherited two other houses that she divided into apartments and rented to several tenants.

At first, when I went to Nichole's, she was either engaged in her Jane Fonda Aerobics Workout of which she was a religious follower, or hunched over a desk littered with gas, electric and plumbing bills. In addition to managing her rented houses, Nichole had arranged all the maintenance and paid the bills for Cosmo's restaurant, and had worked as the hostess at night. I wondered how she ever got any painting done, but she had several studios, one in the loft of the Miller Hill house, one above Cosmo's restaurant, and one at Days Studios. Nichole was not extravagant; she was just prolific. She liked to work on several paintings at once, and her canvases were so enormous she occupied the space in all three studios. She was always threatening to move out of the studios at Days and Cosmo's and only work at home, but she was afraid if she did she would never leave the house.

After Nichole met Frank and he started working on the house, it was consumed with hammering and sawing. The entire back of the house next to Nichole's bedroom was opened up so the place looked like a stage set. Nichole was always on her hands and knees hammering, all dusty, wearing a pair of jeans, her hair tied up in a scarf.

After she told her father about Frank, Nichole had quit working for her father at the restaurant. She said he had ranted and raved, yelled and screamed, called her a whore and public disgrace to the family, told her she was never any good, that she had always let him down, time after time, and this was the final act, the last straw. She said that he saw his own history repeating itself. When I had asked her if Frank was still married, she told me it was not a condition that went away suddenly. When I asked her what she would do next, she said she planned to move out of her studios at Days and Cosmo's to save money, paint at home and live off her rental monies. She said she didn't have time to paint anyway, because she was helping Frank with the house. Since then I had only seen her once, at the Costume Ball, and by then nothing had changed.

When I arrived at Nichole's that day, Frank's truck was not parked in front, and I could not hear any hammering or sawing. Perhaps they had won against the termites and finished the new porch foundation, or maybe they had given up, and Frank had gone back to his wife. Anything could happen in a couple of days.

From the door I could hear Nichole's Jane Fonda Aerobics tape, and Nichole counting and grunting while she labored under the exercises. I pounded on the door as hard as I could and yelled Nichole's name.

"That's the way the Fire Department knocks," Nichole said when she let me in.

The house looked alarmingly tidy. No walls were ripped out; no hammers or nails lay anywhere; no dust from sawn wood or splinters from shingles covered the floor. No rags or work clothes were thrown haphazardly into chairs. Even Nichole's desk was clear from the stacks of bills and ledgers she was usually working with.

"I didn't know you were going to be part of Benefit Week," Nichole said while she was pouring me a glass of cranberry juice.

"What?"

"I saw your house on TV this morning."

"Wasn't that wild?" I said.

"Harper's penchant for exits in helicopters is a theatrical urge."

"Have I ever disagreed with you?" I said.

"It's a double edged sword. The same charm that creates his image serves to undermine it. You know what I mean?"

"When did you become a media analyst?" I said.

"This morning when I watched your house on TV."

I sat down quietly at the kitchen table and drank the

cranberry juice. Even this room was unusually clean. No dishes loitered in the sink; no sugar granules were scattered on the table; the floor looked as if it had just been mopped and polished; everything on the shelves was in its proper place. I wondered how Nichole could have become so fastidious. Perhaps it was Frank's influence.

"So what's happening with Frank?" I asked when we moved into the living room and took our places—me at the dining room table and Nichole in her overstuffed chair by the south window.

"He's negotiating with his wife."

"How does it look?"

"Bad. He might stay with her." Nichole looked down glumly into her juice glass, and then began to turn it slowly in her hand. It seem as if Nichole believed, perhaps for the first time, that Frank would stay with his wife. She looked resigned, almost chastened. Perhaps this explained why everything was in order, nothing left to be cleaned, no bills left to be paid, nothing standing out that needed to be put away, as if the house had been tidied and left for an incoming tenant.

"Why don't you get out?" I said.

"Out of town?"

"Out of the relationship with Frank."

"I think I'd rather leave town."

"You could reconcile with your father before Frank makes a decision."

Nichole got up and began to walk around the room, taking her juice with her. First she went over to the desk and looked at the empty blotting pad and calculator. Then she accosted the tape player, popped the Jane Fonda tape out, flipped it over, and put it back in place again. She approached the south window and looked out. "I don't want to reconcile with my father. Why do you want me to reconcile with my father? He wants me to apologize to him in public. Well, I won't."

"What about the Bocce Tournament? Can't you come with us, judge it, see him, and not apologize?"

"No. He will take it as an unconditional surrender, and so will everyone else. And what difference does it make if I'm at the Bocce Tournament?"

"Well, you can't stay cooped up in this house forever. You are going to end up like one of those old ladies in Oakland who gets caught keeping twenty 20 dogs and cats locked in their house for eight years without ever leaving to empty the garbage. Anyway, we need all three of us to judge the tournament—you, me and Whitney."

Nichole sat in her overstuffed chair again, set her glass on the end table and sighed. She had an air of resignation about her, not just concerning Frank, but about life in general, as if her spirit had been broken, and she could not pretend any longer.

"Whitney is a dyke now," she said. "You've started a fad. Whitney is hanging around with lesbians."

"Well, we're not *all* gay. *You're* not gay. *I'm* not gay."

"I hear you drove a lesbian to Boston," she said. "Overnight."

"It's true."

"Did you sleep with her?"

"She won't have me."

"That'll be the day," she said. "So since when have you been hanging around with lesbians?"

"I drove her to Boston," I said. "Her mother was dying."

"Oh, so now she's a charity case?"

"She didn't want me to do her any favors—I insisted. But I didn't sleep with her."

Nichole threw her hands up and let them fall on the arms of the easy chair.

"You!" she said. "You! You'd sleep with a woman if you felt like it. You'd sleep with anyone you wanted. You! You're pan-sexual! Ubiquitous! Ambidextrous! Omnipresent! Polymorphously perverse! You're a nymphomaniac!" Nichole got up again and began to pace around the room, without pretending to have any purpose except to vent her aggravation.

"Okay, okay," I said. "You've made your point."

"Look, I'm sorry, Kate, but we're really just too different."

"Too different to judge the Bocce Tournament?"

"Too different to be friends."

"What?" I said. "You stop painting, you stop going out, you won't see anyone, you're threatening to leave town, and now we're not friends?"

"I'm sorry, Kate. This town has just gone too far. I have to get out of here. It used to be just fishermen and painters."

I was too caught up in my own crimes to see what the town had to do with it. "I sleep with a few people," I said. "Whitney takes up with a woman, and you don't want to be friends anymore?"

Nichole let her jaw drop in disgust, then closed her mouth and cocked her head when she looked at me, as if she knew better. "A few people?" she said. "You sleep with more people in a week that I've slept with in my lifetime. And Whitney didn't just *take up* with Elaine Barry; you took her to Paradiso's and introduced her! Don't you think I know? You corrupted her. You're friends with that dyke bartender. And then, the crowning insult, you take my father's side and ask me to grovel at his feet in public."

Nichole went into the kitchen and poured more cranberry juice. I turned in my chair to follow her movements.

"I don't believe this," I shouted from the other room. "I really don't believe it. So this means I can't come over? I can't come visit you anymore?"

"It doesn't matter," she said, with that same resignation she had shown in her expression, in her movements, in the fastidiousness of the house. "I'll probably leave town anyway."

She brought the juice jar in, and poured me a glass. I looked up at her from where she was sitting. It seemed a shame to lose such a good friend, such a smart, witty friend. And for a moment I wished I had not known Mary; that I had not taken Whitney to Paradiso's to hear Christianne sing; that I had not slept with so many men. It occurred to me that I might tell Nichole about my amnesia, and set the whole thing straight again; but then I decided no, it would not solve anything. Nichole was too smart for that. She could see right away that, though the amnesia might be real, it was just an excuse. Gabe knew as much and he did not even know what the problem was.

Nichole was back in the easy chair now, with a new glass of juice in her hand.

"My father did exactly what I'm doing now. But was he criticized and shunned? Of course not. He managed to get sympathy out of it. They thought he was arty, compassionate, and he did what his heart told him to do, so people felt sorry for him. Then he became a legend and those people wanted to be his friend, so they came to the restaurant. Everything works in his favor. He can do whatever he wants, and it'll work in his favor."

"He wants to reconcile with you, and you won't. That's not working in his favor."

"He never wanted me. He wanted a son. He wanted someone to run the restaurant. That's why he brought Getz in from Rhode Island and brought Dominic into the restaurant after Dom's father died. If his son had done what I've done, it would be a whole different story. Anyway, I hated the restaurant: all the pettiness and gossip and intrigue, everyone treating you some fake way because you're the boss' daughter, kissing your ass because you're the boss' daughter, wanting to sleep with you because you're the boss' daughter. I should have never come back here when I inherited this house. I should have stayed in New York, where people don't know me from when I was five. Where people aren't petty and vicious. Where people don't know I'm my father's daughter."

I did not know what to say. I had never lost someone before by their own volition. I got up. I had to leave; I was already late for the Bocce Tournament.

***

The inside of Animus Pizza seemed too small to accommodate all the different foods it served and the various clientele it housed. The entire right side of the room was used to prepare the food. The pizza was made in the front by the window and set out on the counters to cool. This was also where, in the morning, the pastries and croissants were laid out. Behind the pizza area was the soda fountain, with its freezers of ice cream, taps for soda and pumps for syrup. The espresso machine sat on the serving counter. On the walls above the food area Joe Houston had painted a mural of little devils, with horns, tails and pitchforks. The devils sat on a wall in various attitudes, some with one leg slung casually over the wall, some holding their pitchforks upright, others glaring straight at the viewer so that at times it startled the customers, who mistook them for real people in costumes. The sky Joe had painted around the devils was such a pale, celestial blue, and the clouds so close and wispy and ethereal, it seemed that the devils had taken over Heaven. If you asked Joe if this was what he meant by it, he would just stroke his black signature glove and chuckle evasively.

The other half of Animus Pizza was occupied by booths and video machines. The walls above the booths were used as gallery space to house photography shows. In the back of the pizza parlor, a door led out to the rear patio and yard. In the very back, there was a bocce court, made professionally by real Italians, and smoothed down with an authentic cement roller machine, the kind that was used to pave streets. The three brothers who owned Animus Pizza were serious bocce players, and very proud of their court. They said it was the only legitimate court on Cape Cod.

When I arrived at Animus Pizza, a crowd had already gathered to watch the bocce tournament to benefit the Harper Martin Defense Fund. They seemed to be mainly tourists; I did not recognize anyone who was standing outside on the front patio, watching the skateboarders perform their leaps, twirls and dives off the curb.

The TV camera crews had also arrived. The vans were parked out front, with their right wheels up on the curb, to leave room for the traffic on the narrow street. They were laying out cables everywhere, in the front door, through the pizza parlor and out the back, along the side yards and across the front patio. The cables created quite an obstacle course for the skateboarders who were jumping over them.

The tourists seemed to be just as interested in the camera crews as they were in the upcoming bocce game. Many of them were inspecting the camera and lighting equipment, playing with the microphones and talking to crew members. Perhaps they weren't so interested in the bocce game or Harper Martin as they were in being on the spot where some media event was happening, the way people rush to a fire or airplane crash or other accident. Or maybe they wanted to see themselves on the evening news.

I wove my way through the crowd, trying to get inside the pizza parlor, and then beyond it to the backyard, where I thought I would find Joe Houston and Whitney. Some of the people I passed were dressed as Harper Martin, in beige chinos, white shirts, string ties, leather jackets and fedoras. Others were dressed in Mayan ball player costumes: naked except for a belt around the waist with a flap hanging down in front, a stone chest plate, leather straps laced up their arms and legs.

The crowd was so thick I could hardly move through it. I had reached the Space Invaders machine when something stopped me. It was a smell, that talc-y smell. It was Grace.

"Borrowed anyone's car lately?" Grace said.

I thought Grace was referring to my trips down to New York to deliver Harper's statements to Dan Rather at the CBS News. Then it occurred to me that, after that morning's broadcast of Harper surrendering himself to the Feds from my skylight, the whole town probably knew I was Deep Throat, the Informant.

"No," I said.

"You haven't borrowed anyone's car? Not even someone's who might have needed it to drive to Boston and see her mother before she died?"

"Oh that," I said, relieved that Grace did not know I was the informant. Then I realized what she meant.

Grace was a friend of Mary's and she was mad because, after I had driven Mary to Boston and we'd both come back again, Mary loaned me her car. Mine was broken. I didn't return it promptly and in the meantime Mary's mother died. If she had had her car, she would have been able to get back up there in time. But I had her car.

"Oh that!" Grace had been saying. "Oh that! As if it doesn't even matter that your carelessness prevented Mary from ever seeing her mother again. As if it doesn't matter that you let Mary buy your drinks, take you out, give you her car to use, and then you take it when she needs it most, sleep with eight different Joes while she's gone, and when she comes back into town you don't even bother to go see her, or call her up on the phone even. I can't believe it. You oughta be locked up. Kate! Kate! Are you listening to me?"

When I looked up again, I was standing in the backyard near the bocce court with Joe Houston. Joe was wearing the traditional Mayan ball player's costume: a belt around his waist with flaps hanging down the front and back, a stone chest plate made from paper maché, leather straps up his arms and legs, and a special leather pouch to carry his Gauloises cigarettes.

"How'd I get out here?" I said.

"You walked out with me," he said.

"But where's Grace? Wasn't I with Grace?"

"We left her in there," he said. "Are you epileptic?"

"I don't think so."

"Because Grace was talking to you, and you didn't seem to hear any of it, and now you don't even remember how you got outside." He put his hand on my shoulder, as if to make the news more palatable.

"It was too crowded inside. I couldn't get enough air."

"Maybe you're claustrophobic then."

"Maybe." I looked him up and down, scrutinizing his costume as if I had not seen it yet.

Elaine and Whitney came up to us at the court. "Aren't we supposed to judge this game?" Whitney said. "Where's Nichole?" She looked around. Whitney had on reflector Vuarnet sunglasses and she had just gotten out of the shower. Her hair, which she hennaed, had been turning a rust color, but now its seemed to be headed toward a shade of magenta. She was wearing her signature white t-shirt with the tiger lithoed on the front, and her tiger-striped knee socks.

"She's not coming," I said. "And it's not your fault, Whitney."

"It doesn't matter," Elaine said. "She'll blame herself."

"I said forget it! Forget it!" Whitney yelled, and walked closer to the bocce court.

"She's had some bad news," Elaine explained when Whitney was out of earshot.

Some of the players had assembled and were practicing pitching the balls from one end of the court at the stationery ball at the other end. Whitney stood watching them. I came up and stood next to her. "I think somebody better tell me how this game is played," she said, "before I have to judge it." I explained that each player tried to get his ball as close to the stationary ball as he could without touching it. I said if there were any dispute as to which ball was closest, we would have to rule on it. Then I confessed I had never really played, and had just learned the rules from Joe.

Whitney nodded, and watched the players again. Then she asked me if they could knock each others' balls out of position. "Now you're catching on," Joe said. He had come up from behind and was standing between us.

"I'm not sure you want us to judge this thing, Joe," Whitney said. "Neither one of us has played. It's like the blind leading the blind."

"That's the way of life," he said.

"Mr. Eastern Philosophy," Whitney said.

So the official game started. Whitney and I judged it as best we could. While the teams were playing, the tourists wandered around the backyard and pizza parlor, drinking sodas, shakes and coffee, eating pizza and ice cream. The camera crews filmed the game, and stopped the tourists from eating in order to ask them what they thought about Harper Martin and the Nicaragua question, or about their costume, their background, their home town, their reasons for attending benefit week.

After the game was over everybody continued eating and drinking, the TV crews kept on with their interviews. It wasn't the bocce game that mattered, it was the party; the game was just an excuse to have one.

Joe made me a complimentary chocolate egg cream to thank me for my participation. We took a booth with Whitney and Elaine, who were drinking espressos, and the four of us watched the crowd. Joe took a pack of Gauloises out of the special leather pouch he was wearing on his hip for that purpose, and Elaine lit it for him against the tip of the Player's she was smoking with her coffee.

"So tell us some good news, Whitney," I said, "if you won't tell us the bad."

"There isn't any good news," she said. Judging the bocce Tournament had not distracted her from her gloomy self-absorption.

"There is, too," Elaine said. She and Whitney glared at each other. "I'll tell them myself if you don't."

"Alright," Whitney said. She pushed her espresso cup to the middle of the table. Joe leaned forward and looked into it, then he looked at me as if he were astonished at what he had read there.

"A CBS camera crew came to Days Studios today," Whitney said. "They're working on a profile of Harper Martin, for one of those Special Reports. They interviewed me, and they filmed my studio."

"And the *Incident in Fialta* was mounted on the wall when they did it," Elaine said, triumphant. "They filmed that, too." She beamed at me, and took another drag on her cigarette.

Whitney worked in primary colors mostly, but lately she had added black. *Incident in Fialta* was a diptych that had to be mounted in a corner of her studio at Days so the canvases were perpendicular to each other, making an L-shape on the two walls. The canvases were six-by-six feet and filled with swirling cyclone shapes that set sparks flying in arcs across the canvas. It looked very much like an incident.

"*The Incident in Fialta*!" I said. "On the National news!"

"Congratulations," Joe said gravely, and reached over the table to shake her hand.

"So now can you tell us the bad news?" I said.

Whitney and Elaine looked at each other. "I guess not," Whitney said. Whitney brought her cup toward her and looked down into it. When Joe asked her if she wanted another one on the house, she nodded. So Joe got up, brought two espressos back, and set them in front of Elaine and Whitney. Then he and Elaine lit fresh cigarettes.

"Your *Incident in Fialta* on national television," I said.

"You were on National television this morning, don't forget," Whitney said. "Well, your house anyway, and your, your—" Whitney looked at Joe and suddenly seemed guilty.

"Go ahead, say it," Joe said. "Her *Joe*. But it wasn't Joe at all, was it, darling?" Joe said it to me with mock sweetness, put his arm around me as best he could with his chest plate on, and kissed me.

"So when is this Special Report going to air?" I said.

"You mean the profile on Harper Martin?" Joe said.

"In a few days, I think," Whitney said.

"I've never seen you jealous before, Joe," Elaine said. She reached across the table to light another Gauloise for him, then watched him take a drag on the cigarette. Joe exhaled, stroked his glove, and returned her look.

"I told you, Elaine, I'm a mysterious guy."

While Elaine and Whitney teased Joe about being jealous, I looked around the room. Some of the skateboarders had come inside, and were playing the Space Invaders machine, with their skateboards propped up against their legs. At the espresso machine the tourists had surrounded a few of the bocce players and were fingering their chest plates, leather skirts and lace up sandals. The TV camera crews were shining spotlights on the bocce players, and trying to interview them, but the crowd kept getting in the way, and the players really couldn't hear the questions in all the noise, so they just squinted into the bright lights, smiled, and showed off their headdresses.

The Mother of the Year had just arrived and was standing in the entranceway, dressed in the most outrageous costume. She was Tlacolteotl, the Goddess of Sin, as that deity had been shown in pictures from the Codex Borbonicus on one of Dan Rather's Temple of the Jaguar Reports. She was wearing a skirt that had mussels and small crabs sewn onto the fabric. A belt of fish heads was wrapped around her waist several times, so it criss-crossed and draped her hips. She was barefoot, and wore bracelets of shark's teeth around her ankles and wrists. Her hair was tied up in a white muslin turban. On the front of it was a brass pendant of two snakes, their necks intertwined and their jaws locked on each other so their fangs collided. A halter-top made from the same white muslin as the turban was wrapped around her chest like a gauze bandage, leaving her stomach and shoulders bare.

Cosmo appeared in the doorway, disappeared in the crowd around the Mother of the Year, and then reappeared by the Space Invaders machine. Joe motioned him over to the table. "I thought you were going to play on our team," Joe said.

Cosmo shook hands with Joe and Elaine, then stood in front of the booth, looking around at all of us as if he were assessing our worth. Whitney and Elaine moved in to make room for Cosmo on their side of the booth. He sat down and then looked around at the crowd as if he were trying to locate a waiter to serve him. "Well, I'm sorry I missed Nichole," he said. "When did she leave?"

Joe and Whitney looked at me. I said Nichole didn't come. "It's my fault," Whitney said. Elaine took the cigarette out of her mouth and made a clucking noise.

"No, it's my fault," I said.

"You're very kind, both of you," Cosmo said. Obviously he thought we were just being polite, and he was really to blame.

When Cosmo looked around again for a waiter, Joe took the opportunity to look suspiciously at me. Then Joe asked Cosmo if he would like something to drink.

"A slice please, thank you, Joe," he said, and continued to look around distractedly.

After Joe left Elaine shot me inquiring glances and Whitney appeared bewildered. Finally Elaine said she wanted to get a closer look at the Goddess of Sin, and asked Whitney to go with her. Cosmo let them out of the booth. When they were gone, he sat back down again and said to me: "I'm really sorry I'm late. At the last minute I had to check in a wine shipment. I was afraid I'd miss her."

I looked down into the dregs of Whitney's espresso cup. Perhaps he had arrived late on purpose, so if Nichole had come he would have appeared nonchalant. And he would have made her wait.

"She really didn't come at all?" Cosmo said. He didn't seem to believe this.

Joe brought Cosmo's slice of pizza to the table on a napkin, told them he had been asked by the reporters to pose in his Mayan ball player's costume with the Goddess of Sin, and left to be photographed. Cosmo turned to watch him go, as if he wished he could be Joe at that moment instead of himself, with Joe's looks and occupations, Joe's circumstances and history, Joe's own set of gossip and rumor, legend and myth.

"I went over to the house and talked to her this morning," I said. "She got mad at me. I'm the wrong person to try to help anyone. I think I just made things worse."

"That's kind," Cosmo said.

He ate his pizza while I watched quietly, affording him his private thoughts. He could have been wishing that he had never had an affair with Nello's wife, that he had never been so attentive to Dominic and Getz, never treated them like sons, that he had involved more deeply Nichole in the restaurant business. Maybe he was dreaming of the reconciliation between them, of his daughter breaking her resolve and coming to him in tears. But maybe not. Perhaps he was wishing that he had run off with Nello's wife instead of relinquishing her and staying with his own, that Dominic and Getz were in fact his own sons. In any case, he had come today to see his daughter. He had arrived late to preserve his dignity, and now he was there, sitting in the booth with me, eating a slice of pizza. His daughter hadn't come.

I wanted to suggest that he go to Nichole's house and talk to her, that he make a gesture toward her, but I didn't know how to circumvent his pride to make the idea seem tenable. Nichole was only doing what he had once done; maybe she was a lot like him; but I had tried that argument at the restaurant, and it seemed to be part of what was bothering him.

He finished eating his slice of pizza and wiped his hands on a napkin. "You could go over there," I said. "To her house. Something. You know."

"I know," he said. He wadded up the napkin and dropped it in Elaine's ashtray, then he reached across the table and clasped my shoulder. People were always trying to comfort me. He slid out of the booth, brushed the crumbs off his pants and looked around. "I have to get back," he said.

After Cosmo left, I stretched out on my side of the booth and watched the proceedings. Joe was still posing with the Mother of the Year, though the TV crews had stopped filming. A reporter was tapping on Joe's black glove and asking him what it meant. At the soda fountain Grace was talking with Elaine and Whitney. The skateboarders had abandoned the video machines and gone back outside to stage another exhibition on the front patio.

Elaine sat down in the booth with me. She had left Whitney at the counter with Grace. I watched Grace yell and gesticulate wildly. Whitney was nodding sympathetically and trying to break in to explain something, but Grace would not let her. Whitney waited patiently, and then tried again.

"So what's the bad news?" I said.

Elaine lit a Player and removed Cosmo's napkin from her ashtray. "Whitney told her parents she has a girlfriend."

"Jesus Christ," I said.

"My sentiments exactly."

I shook my head. "So what did they say? How did they take it?" I looked at Elaine and reconsidered. "Maybe you shouldn't tell me. Maybe I don't want to know."

"They refuse to ever see or talk to her again."

"Charming," I said. "They disown their only daughter at the age of 30, because she has a girlfriend. Stunning. Expert. That's just perfect."

"You're angry."

"Angry! Of course, I'm angry!" I reached out for Elaine's cigarette.

"What?" Elaine said, pulling it away.

"Give me the cigarette."

"You don't smoke."

"I do now. I want the cigarette. Give me the cigarette."

Elaine watched me suspiciously for a moment, then slowly passed the cigarette over to me. I took a long drag and let the smoke out. "You're smoking a cigarette," she said. "You don't smoke. You're smoking a cigarette." I took another long drag. I watched the smoke curl up off the burning tip. Elaine reached for it, but I pulled away, so Elaine took out another one and lit it.

"So how is she taking it?" I said. "Is she hurt?"

"She's stunned. She thought they'd be upset, but she didn't have any idea they would ostracize her. How are you taking it?"

I twirled the cigarette in the ashtray. "Me? I'm her friend. I'm mad as hell."

"But you're not blaming yourself, are you?"

"Why not? Nichole already blames me. Add it to the list."

"The list?"

"I deprived Mary of her last visit to her dying mother; I've ostracized Whitney from her family. It's a list."

"Oh, you mean Grace," she said. She chuckled. "Don't worry about her. She's just jealous."

"Jealous?"

"Sure. It's just a little Dyke Drama. She thinks Mary would get involved with her if she wasn't interested in you. But she wouldn't. Mary's never gone for anyone her own age."

"Interested in me? Mary's not interested in me. Mary could care less about me. She never acts like she likes me. She doesn't like me."

Elaine squinted behind the smoke from her cigarette. "She let you drive her to her parents' house."

"Nothing happened!"

Elaine laughed. "Calm down. Nobody said anything happened. Mary's friends just know what it means. *What it means.* You see? And Grace is jealous."

"Jealous?"

Elaine laughed again, put out her cigarette, and lit another one. She leaned back in the booth. "I'm telling you this so you won't let Grace bother you. But I see you're just more upset. I thought you were tougher than that."

"Tough as nails. Hard as a ball bearing."

"Come on, Kate. Lighten up. Whitney has a problem. Cosmo has a problem. My brothers have a problem. You do not have a problem. Mary has befriended you, and you're taking some flack for it. That's all."

"That's all. Dyke Drama."

"Now you're catching on," she said.

I finished my cigarette and rubbed out the cinder in the ashtray. "So is Whitney going to be alright?" I said. "What can we do?"

"She'll be alright. It won't help if you go blaming yourself."

"Hey, why would I blame myself when I have Nichole to do it for me?"

Elaine shook her head. "I thought you were tougher than this," she repeated. She got up. "Mary's back from Boston, you know."

"I know."

"You should go see her."

She went back to the counter and left with Whitney. The Mother of the Year had retired to the back yard. Some reporters were filming her around the bocce court. Joe had returned to the soda fountain, and was trying to keep his chest-plate out of the way while he scooped ice cream cones.

I climbed out of the booth and stood in line at the soda fountain. When I reached the counter, Joe winked at me, and made me a chocolate egg cream without asking me what I wanted. He held the cup at eye level and inspected the foam. "A work of art," he said, handing it to me.

I thanked him. "Hey, you," he said. "What do you say we go to my house, watch the news, catch the Temple of the Jaguars Special Report, grab a bite, and then run down to the Fashion Show at Grace's Djellaba store? Whatta you say?"

"I have to work."

"You don't have to work," he said. "It's Benefit Week."

"I don't know."

"Come on. I'll make you dinner."

He came around the soda fountain, took me by the elbow, and led me toward the door. Joshua skateboarded into the pizza parlor, executed a triple spin, and catapulted off the backyard porch. When both he and his skateboard were in the air, he kicked the board into his hand and landed flat on both feet on the backyard lawn like a gymnast executing a dismount. The crowd cheered. Then he saw me and Joe walking away.

"Gotta light?" he yelled at me. "Hey Kate, I *said*, Gotta light?"

***

Joe's apartment was more like a painting studio with a bathroom than a place to live. The large rectangular room with high ceilings and north windows had no furniture except for a mattress on the floor with some clothes thrown over it for bedding, and a card table in the middle of the space filled with tin cans holding brushes and sticks, jars and tubes of paint, and assorted metal lids. The television sat on the floor at the foot of the mattress, plugged into the socket inside the bathroom—the only electrical outlet on the walls.

"You live here?" I said.

Joe turned the TV on. "Only in summer," he said.

He explained that he could not afford the summer rates on his apartment, so he sublet it and had moved into this, his painting studio, for the season. He was at work all day and all night anyway, and just came there between Animus and the Bad Attitude to watch the CBS news and Temple of the Jaguars Report. Then he went back to work.

"Your landlord doesn't charge you year-round rates?" I said.

"Why would he charge me year-round what he can get from a tourist for the summer? There's no more year round rates. Just summer and winter."

"I have year-round rates."

"Well hang onto the place. There aren't going to be anymore year-round rentals in a few years. The whole town's getting gentrified, like Soho. Like the Lower East Side."

The minute I began to wonder where the promised dinner was hidden, Joe recognized the bewildered look on my face, went into the bathroom, opened the small refrigerator underneath the sink, and pulled out a giant cracked crab and a bottle of White Zinfandel. He brought them out to me, and set them down at my feet, where I was sitting on the mattress. Then he pulled a pair of jeans under the plate to serve as a tablecloth.

"Where did you get this?" I asked, pointing to the crab.

"The fridge," he said. He went to the coat closet and pulled out a loaf of French bread.

"Before that?"

"Alaska. Alaskan King Crab."

He went over to the card table, fiddled in the tin cans of brushes and sticks, and brought back a plastic scraping tool, a wooden mallet and a twisted wire.

"You're living in a fishing village; you've got ocean on three sides of you, and you buy Alaskan King Crab?"

"We don't have crabs here. Not big crabs." He held his arms wide apart, as if he were about to embrace someone, to show me the size of the crab he wanted. Then, using the twisted wire, he extracted the cork from the bottle of White Zinfandel.

"But we have lobster, squid, cod, scallops ..."

"People always want what they can't have, don't they?" he said gently. Then he poured the wine into what appeared to be a paint mixing cup—the sawed off bottom of a quart milk carton.

"I guess so," I said.

Joe showed me how to use the soft wooden mallet and plastic prying tool to break the crab shells open and pull the meat out. Then he went back to the card table and found me a sharp stick to use as a fork, in case I did not want to hold the crab meat in my fingers. When he was halfway back to the mattress, he returned to the card table, found a second stick, and brought them both back to me. I could use them like chopsticks if I wanted.

"Crab from Alaska, wine from California, French bread, a nutcracker and chopsticks. I'm confused," I said. "Where are we?"

"In America."

He sat down next to me on the mattress and watched Dan Rather report the *CBS Evening News*. "It's American, this dinner. Mixing everything up, combining cultures. It's patriotic. Don't you think?" He kissed me on the cheek again.

While Joe watched the *CBS Evening News*, I leaned against him, ate crab, drank wine, and looked at the paintings that were in progress along the walls of his studio. They were all done on masonite boards, six feet high and ten feet long. The boards were gessoed white, and painted over with black and red acrylic paint. Only black and red. Figures were etched in to the paint with implements, like crude finger painting. They were nothing like the meticulous *Escher in Instanbul* mural at the Bad Attitude Cinema, or the dreamy *Devils Occupy Heaven* mural above the soda fountain at Animus Pizza.

Joe grabbed my arm and shook it. "Look, Kate, Kate," he said. "There's your house. There's your skylight. There's Harper surrendering himself to the Federal Marshal."

I watched the footage of Harper climbing out of the skylight and falling into the arms of the helicopter pilot. I barely recognized the scene. It didn't look anything like what had happened that morning, what I heard, what I saw, what I remembered. The sound of the helicopter had frightened me. The house shook like an earthquake. Harper might have fallen off the roof. Harper might never be coming back. He had said, *Remember what we talked about*, and I couldn't remember. I felt guilty. I had stolen the skin-suit man. Then the reporters had swarmed my apartment, beating on the doors, and I had hidden inside the bed, underneath the covers, after piling the furniture against the door to keep them out. It was like a siege.

But this television broadcast of the event looked pleasant enough. Sure, it was exciting, slightly dangerous, but in a glamorous way, the way James Bond dangling from the Eiffel Tower in a 007 movie was dangerous. James Bond would never really fall off the roof, but Harper might. James Bond would always film a sequel, but Harper might not come back.

"Look, Kate, he's climbing into the copter. He's waving to the crowd. Kate, Kate the crowd's cheering. Where were you? Inside, watching on TV?" I just looked at him. What if they put Harper in jail? What if he never came back? What had we talked about that I was supposed to remember? "Kate, why don't you answer me?"

"The questions you're asking, they aren't even in English."

I stood up and went over to the walls to examine his paintings at close range.

Joe took me by the shoulders and pulled me back, away from the paintings.

"You're too close," he said. "You can't see anything so close. You don't have any perspective. Stand here. What do you think the room is so big for?"

On the television, Dan Rather was saying that sources close to the federal government had revealed that negotiations had begun between Harper Martin and Federal representatives, but no other information was forthcoming.

"These are so different than your murals," I said.

"So, are you bummed?" He stroked his black signature glove.

"No, I like them. They're just different."

"I'm a versatile guy. Full of surprises." He put his arms around me. "You know, when Harper gets released he's gonna have to go to the Getty Museum and paint that replica of the Temple of the Jaguars mural."

"Yeah, so?"

"Well, maybe he'll need help. Maybe he can't do it all by himself. Did you ever think of that?"

"No."

"Kate, Kate, you're not thinking. You never think."

It was true. "Will he really get released?" I said.

We returned to the mattress and finished eating.

"Harper? Are you kidding? They have to release him."

"Why?"

"Because everyone loves him. Haven't you been watching the news?"

"I *am* watching the news."

"Well look," Joe said, pointing to the television. Dan Rather was reporting that sentiment against United States intervention in Central America was growing. He showed film clips of protestors demonstrating in Providence and New Haven with signs that said: *FREE HARPER MARTIN*, *U.S. OUT OF CENTRAL AMERICA* and *WE DON'T WANT ANOTHER VIETNAM*. "The man's a genius. He has Rock Star status now, like the President or the Pope."

"Rock Star status?"

"Sure," he said. He poured the rest of the wine into my milk carton cup, tore off a piece of French bread and offered it to me. "The Pope used to just be a Pope. You know, a religious figure. The head of the Catholic Church. But now you see him on TV in front of all those hordes of people. It's like he's giving a rock concert or something. He's a star now. He's a media figure, like a rock star. He's got Rock Star status, same as the President."

The news was over. Joe threw the remains of the French bread into the coat closet, the wine bottle and crab shells into the trash. Someone knocked on the door. Joe opened it and the Flower Man walked in. "Kate?" he said. "Delivery for you." He handed me a yellow rose.

"What does yellow mean?" Joe said. "Jealousy?"

I took the rose and read the note, which said, *You're not trying.* I asked Joe if it were from him.

"Me? Would I send roses to my own apartment?"

"One rose," I said. "To your studio." I looked at the note again. *You're not trying.* Obviously it made some reference to something I was supposed to be trying to do. But was it something I could remember, or something that had happened at night? Was it a reference to what Harper and I had discussed the night before he turned himself in?

While I brooded over the note, Joe asked the Flower Man if he could ship roses long distance, or if they would wilt before they arrived.

"Go to the florist here," I said. "They'll call a florist in the town you want them delivered, and that other florist will send them fresh." I was beginning to have a hunch who the note was from.

"What if there's no florist where these roses are going?"

"Who ever heard of a place with no florist?"

"What about a jungle? A desert? A swamp? A rain forest? What about a jail?"

"You've made your point," I said. I looked at the note again. Gabe had asked me if I would see only him. I said I would try.

"Thank you," Joe said. The Flower Man told him that he could sleep a rose for three days if he put the stem on ice, and for three weeks if he put the entire rose on ice. To wake the rose up again he had to put the stem in hot water. "And then how long will it last?" Joe said. The Flower Man told him the life span of a rose was about two weeks: three days to open, nine days to expand and two days to die.

"The life span of a rose," I said, snapping at the note with my fingers. How did Gabe know where I was at this very moment?

"Three weeks on ice, that's not very long," Joe said. He seemed to be considering it.

"Six months is the longest I've ever slept a rose," the Flower Man said. "But that's very complicated."

"Well thanks," Joe said to the Flower Man. "I'll get back to you."

"Sure thing," the Flower Man said.

After the Flower Man left, Joe turned off the TV and sat down on the mattress next to me. He took the note out of my hand and read it. "You don't know who sent this?" he said.

"I know," I said. I put the note in my pocket.

"Are you okay? You're always so distracted and fidgety."

"I'm sorry."

Just then Grace walked in the door. She trembled so much her white hair vibrated like a nimbus around her face. "I just want you to know that I hate you," she said to me. "I despise you, I wish you were never born, I wish you had never come to this town."

"Oh Christ," Joe said.

"You think you can just waltz into this town without the faintest idea of what's going on, do whatever you goddamn please, have whomever you goddamn want, and then walk away from it without a complaint out of anyone. But it doesn't work that way around here. If you screw someone over you pay. And *you* screw everyone over. You make everyone miserable. What do you think this is, a side show? A spectator sport? These are our lives, and you're just watching, and cashing in, you're just toying with people. You don't have any *real* feelings. I wish you would leave and never come back. Why don't you just leave, leave us all in peace."

"Alright, Grace," Joe said.

"I hope you get what you deserve," Grace added, and walked out the door.

Joe put his gloved hand on my arm. "You shouldn't let her upset you. She's just acting out. They taught her that in AA."

"Can I have a cigarette?" I said, motioning to the pack of Gauloises on the bed.

"You don't smoke."

"I do now," I said, reaching across him toward the pack.

He pulled away. "You told me you made a vow when your mother died, that you would never smoke."

"I did?"

"Kate, you told me your mother had died of lung cancer, that she was like a female Humphrey Bogart, a real stormy, brooding person, like a volcano about to erupt, and that she continued to chain smoke, even when she knew she was dying."

"I don't remember ever telling you that," I said, reaching again for the cigarettes.

Joe kept me at bay. "You talk about your mother all the time! That's practically all you ever talk about. Don't tell me you can't remember?"

I looked at him. I never talked about my mother to anyone. "Please, can I have a cigarette?" I said. Joe shook his head. "It's not a cardinal sin, it's just a cigarette."

Joe sighed and reached for his pack of Gauloises. "I can't believe you're doing this after everything you've told me." He handed me a cigarette. "Look, let me tell you something else, if you feel that bad. Maybe this will make you feel better. Grace is Elaine Barry's ex-girlfriend. That's why she's so mad at you. I mean, you introduced Whitney to Elaine, so now her ex has gone off with someone else because of you. That's all. Don't take it so hard. She doesn't really think you treated Mary bad. She's just jealous."

I reached into my pocket again, and fingered Gabe's note. *You're not trying*, it said. It was true; I wasn't trying. I wasn't even thinking. I got up. "I have to go," I said.

"You shouldn't let Grace wig you out. The Fashion Show's just starting, and you're going to miss the whole thing." I shrugged. "Well then, will you come back to my place afterward?" I said I didn't know. "Will you be alright alone? Should I come with you?" I said I would be alright, and wandered off to look for Gabe.

***

I had to walk through the center of town to reach Cosmo's restaurant. On the way I passed Nello's restaurant, where Cosmo was blamed for stealing Nello's wife and wrecking his marriage; I passed The Bad Attitude Café, where Antaeus was blamed for Mrs. Souza's death; I passed Lili Marleen's, where Getz was blamed for embezzling the old Zanzibar's money and ruining its business; I passed The White Sands, where Raphael Souza was blamed for his wife's suicide and his daughter's murder. By the time I had arrived at Cosmo's, my sense of remorse had weakened in this context, and I did not feel half as guilty as I had when I had left Joe's apartment. But I would confess anyway, just in case Grace was right—the way a dying non-believer prays for forgiveness, just in case there is a God.

When I arrived at Cosmo's restaurant, the patio was filled with tourists who had come to Provincetown to see the Benefit Week activities and were waiting to eat. When the Temple of the Jaguars story broke, the merchants and restaurant owners expected the tourist business would increase; but no one anticipated that this many people would come, except for maybe Harper Martin himself. Some locals were beginning to believe he had planned the whole thing.

I pushed my way through the crowd and into the restaurant. In the front dining room Lance was entertaining some customers by describing the Costume Ball. When I came in he was mimicking the hex that the Voodoo Woman had performed on the reporters.

In the kitchen the order wheel was full of tags, the

waiters ran in and out carrying trays of steaming plates full of mussels and calamari, and Gabe was pouring different sauces into a half dozen plates of pasta at one time. Dominic stood at the hostess station, ringing up bills for the waiters, answering the telephone, seating customers, and even found time to explain to one group of tourists what the upcoming Whale Watch would be like.

"What a mess," I said to Dominic when he was through explaining breeches and dorsal fins to the tourists. "I'm sorry I'm late."

"It's alright," he said. "Gabe told me you weren't coming at all tonight."

"Gabe said I wasn't coming?"

"Yeah, wasn't that the message you gave him?"

The phone rang again. Dominic answered it while he gathered up some menus to seat the next party of four. He led them into the dining room, carrying the phone with him. I wandered into the kitchen, where the waiters were making their own salads and desserts, throwing parsley and lemon wedges onto the plates of shrimp adriatico and stuffed flounder before carrying them out to the customers.

"I hear you've been lying to Dominic about me," I said when Gabe looked up to empty a boiling pot of water into the sink.

"I've been covering your ass so you don't get fired," he said.

I shook my head. He was much too nice to me; I couldn't help but feel guilty. "I got your note," I said. "You should be a private detective."

"Don't flatter yourself," he said. "You're not hard to find. You're too predictable."

Lance came into the kitchen. "Is this jealousy I see, rearing its ugly, tumescent head?"

"Get lost," Gabe said.

"Don't you love the pithy little vignettes that flare up during the summer?" Lance said. He slapped a wedge of ricotta pie onto a plate and left.

"Can we talk after work?" I said. "I think I can tell you the secret now. You know, about the husband stashed in Monte Carlo."

Gabe looked up from the kettle and wiped his face with his apron. "Oh, so you finally admit there's a secret. Well, it's about time. This better be good."

"It is."

I started preparing the salads and filling cannoli shells. Nothing more was said about the matter, but after work, I followed Gabe upstairs to his apartment.

Gabriel Paradise grew up in Chelsea. He studied graphic design at Pratt Institute and planned to go into advertising. But when he realized that the fine arts were hype, that his good looks were hype, that his career in advertising would really be hype, he gave it all up and moved to Provincetown. He waited tables at Cosmo's the first 15 summers and made enough money to go to Greece, Italy and Spain in the winters. Eventually he decided that waiting tables was hype too—women giving him big tips because he was handsome and charming, so he moved into the kitchen, where all he had to complain about was Dominic bossing him around and waitresses kissing him on the neck when he was trying to stir and sieve. He wanted peace, something as simple as that, but there was always bustle and jostling and hype. When it became too much, he went to visit his mother, who lived out on Long Island. When he stayed long enough to realize there was no peace there either, he would pack her discarded televisions, tape players and VCRs into his car and return to Provincetown. Recently he had bought some land on the National Seashore overlooking Hatches Harbor, so his view of open land was assured. He wanted to build a house there. He was certain he could find peace in it.

Gabe's apartment was one of those studios out on the very tip of Cosmo's wharf, above the water-most end of the restaurant. It had a good view of the bay—the coast guard wharf to the east, Long Point to the west. He had made the loft into a bedroom. The best views of the water were from that vantage point. From there he could watch the ferry travel past Hatches Harbor on its way to Boston. Maps of Greece, Italy and Spain hung in the loft; downstairs, posters from Gabe's Pratt Institute days, advertising student exhibitions, were displayed. The refrigerator was stocked with wines from the restaurant, various sauces for pasta and bottles of Tsing Dao beer. Gabe had collected a stereo, cassette player, and television. On his most recent trip to his mother's house, he brought back a VCR.

But the main room had changed since I was last there. A large drafting table had been set up in the middle with a high intensity lamp screwed onto the edge with a vice grip. The table was slanted at a 45-degree angle, and equipped with a T-square that could be fastened and rolled around on its surface. The floor around the table was littered with stencils, ink pens, pencils, erasers, magazine cut outs, and the magazines themselves. Drawings and collages were impaled haphazardly on the wall behind the table. The whole area had a sense of sudden fury about it, as if a crazed genius had been stricken with a truth, and had worked in a frenzy all night to bring it to fruition.

"Wow," I said, "what's all this?"

Gabe opened the refrigerator and took out a Tsing Tao. He fixed a club soda with lime for me, running the lime wedge around the rim of the glass before he dropped it in.

"I've been working," he said.

"But just last night you were glad no one even remembered you were a graphic designer."

I recognized the face on the cover of one of the magazines, and picked it up. It was the current issue of *Newsweek*, which had come out that morning, and the face was Harper Martin's. The caption said, *Auto-SuperStar, or How to Create Your Own Media Event.*

"Is this fake? Did you make this?" I waved the *Newsweek* at him.

Gabe laughed. "No. That's for real. The ones on the wall are mine."

I ran my hands along the wall, inspecting the sketches and cut outs, lifting the leaves of paper to look at the ones underneath. "But just last night you said—"

"I had a change of heart," he said. He handed me the club soda.

I sat down on the floor and began looking at the other magazines. There were copies of *Time*, *Life*, *The New Republic*, *Rolling Stone*, *Interview*, *Gentlemen's Quarterly*, *Vanity Fair*, *Art In America* and *L.A. Style*, and they all had photographs or drawings of Harper Martin on the cover.

"What is this? What's happening?" I said. "Where did you get these? What's going on?"

"It's Wednesday. The shipment of new magazines gets

trucked into Provincetown on Wednesday. I just happened to discover them all this morning, when I was renting movies at Ethan's Pharmacy." He lifted a video cassette off the TV table and showed it to me. "Sir Laurence Olivier in *Othello*. 1965. A controversial performance."

"You sound like the *New York Times*," I said. So he had been to Ethan's Pharmacy and seen Mary. She had been back for a few days now, and according to Raphael and Elaine, she wanted to see me, but I had not been to see her. Gabe, however, had seen her.

"I'm quoting them verbatim."

I looked at all the magazines again. "Jesus Christ," I said.

"You're right, he is beginning to achieve a kind of saintly status. What are the categories of martyrdom—venerable, beatified, and then saint? I think he's at least made it to venerable, don't you?"

"Harper Martin has rock star status, like the Pope," I said, and then realized I was quoting Joe Houston.

Gabe rummaged through the video cassettes he had rented.

"But how can one person be on the cover of so many magazines at one time?" I said.

"It's easy. *Newsweek* and *Time* always have the same cover. *Rolling Stone* and *Interview* always have the same cover. *Vanity Fair* usually has the same cover as *Rolling Stone*, or *Time*. *G.Q.* usually has the same cover as *Vanity Fair* or *Interview*. *L.A. Style* and *Art in America* just jumped into the fray, that's all." Gabe sat down in the easy chair opposite the television. He had selected *Children of Paradise* and the beginning of it was playing with the sound off. Gabe sipped his Tsing Tao and watched the screen.

"Don't you want to hear what I have to say?" I asked.

He looked up at me. "Of course," he said. "But I thought it would add atmosphere to hear your confession with *Children of Paradise* playing in the background. Don't you think it's a nice touch?"

"You always had a bad sense of humor." I wanted to scold him for calling it a confession, but I had used the term myself, so it seemed unfair.

I went to the window and looked out at the water. Lights were flashing everywhere: on the lighthouses at Long Point and Wood End, in the rigging of the fishing trawlers and the decks of the sailboats, on the railing of the coastguard wharf, in the hands of the beachcombers along the shallows. They all seemed to be searching for something.

"Is it hard to say?" Gabe asked. I nodded. "Well, just blurt it out then, no one's watching." He turned his head away from me, toward the television screen.

"I have amnesia about all my sexual experiences," I said. I turned around to look at him. "The doctors call it eroto-amnesia."

It had been going on for about ten years. I would wake up in the morning and I couldn't remember coming home with the guy I was in bed with, couldn't remember anything that had happened the night before, from the time we got into bed until I woke up in the morning. Sometimes when I woke up, I didn't even know where I was.

Once I realized I had this specialized amnesia I refused to tell anyone, and wouldn't let anyone find out about it. I refused to sleep with anyone for more than a night or two, the time it took to build up mutual knowledge, references to the night's conversations, confessions, intimacies. That way I wouldn't have to second-guess the right responses and get caught in a lie. Provincetown suited me because it wasn't unusual to sleep around. But then I met Cedric and a few nights with him was not enough. I stretched it into a month, made too many wrong guesses trying to lie, and had to tell him what was wrong.

He made me see some specialists at the Lahey Clinic in Boston. They recorded my full medical history, submitted me to a battery of tests, tried sleep experiments, hypnosis, even made me stay up all night and have sex during the day. But nothing worked. The minute I went to sleep I forgot it all. They told me I had Sexual Amnesia, one of those illnesses doctors had begun to study but people weren't talking about yet.

Cedric stayed with me for a while, but it was just too desolate for him to think that nothing that happened between us at night mattered, none of it accumulated or lasted, that it was all a waste, forgotten. He started seeing his old girlfriend again and eventually took up with one of the painters at Days Studios. I was afraid the same thing would happen with Gabe if I slept with him more than once. But I was too intrigued by him and unable to stay away. Now I had to tell him.

Compared to some people with the illness, I had been lucky. I had never woken up with injuries, never been robbed, never found myself completely lost. Living in Provincetown helped. I knew who the locals were. The dangers were restricted to the three-mile area of town. Still, I didn't want to go through the same ordeal with Gabe that I had with Cedric.

"Doctors?" Gabe said. He was staring at the television set.

I thought the mention of the doctors would give the

situation some added credibility, but it only seemed to frighten Gabe. "I went to the Lahey Clinic. It's a known condition, but there's nothing they can do. They said sometimes it just goes away."

He still did not look at me. He stared at his knees and twirled the bottle of Tsing Tao in his hands. "So you can't remember anything that's happened between us?" he said. "Nothing at all? You mean you don't even know what it's like?"

For a moment I felt sorry for him, as if I had just realized that he could love and I could not.

He put his beer down on the table and touched the television screen, as if he half-expected to reach in and grab hold of the people inside. Then he withdrew his hand and rested it in his lap. "You haven't told me how the promiscuity fits in," he said. "This story is supposed to explain your promiscuity. Why would you want to sleep with anybody if you can't even remember what happens?"

I told him what the doctors had said—the inability to remember might prevent satisfaction.

He went over to the wall where his sketches were pinned up, and looked at them with distaste, as if they meant something different to him now that I had confessed.

"So why didn't you tell me before?"

"Because I was afraid."

"Then why tell me now? Because of the note I sent you?"

"I've done a lot of things wrong. People are mad at me."

"What have you done? Who's mad?" He almost sounded defensive. I looked out at the water again. The wind had picked up, and all the lights seemed to be frolicking now. "Just blurt it out!"

"Nichole is mad at me because she thinks I take her father's side in their argument, and because I introduced Whitney to a woman who has become her girlfriend."

"Elaine Barry. They came in the restaurant."

"Right. You gave them the VIP treatment."

"You remembered." He smiled sympathetically, as if he realized the joke was not altogether funny. "Go on. What else?"

"I borrowed Mary's car and didn't return it in time for her to see her mother before she died. Grace is mad at me for that, and because I introduced Whitney to Elaine."

"Elaine's her ex."

"Right. Everyone knew but me."

"Is that all?"

I had caused Harper's crates to be confiscated, and I had stolen the skin-suit man, but I couldn't tell him about that.

"And I haven't kept my promise to you," I said.

He stood up and paced around the room for a while. He opened the refrigerator and looked inside, gathered stray shirts off the chairs, picked up some of the magazines and cut outs and arranged them in a neat pile on the floor.

"Do you want to know what I think?" he said. "Do you want to know?" I wasn't sure. "I think you're an egomaniac"—and sat back down in the chair. "All this whining and worrying about your mistakes is a form of egomania, vanity, hubris even—to think you're so important, to think you can have such an effect on people."

"But they are really mad, Gabe."

"Sure they're mad, but not really at *you*. They're just taking it out on you. Grace is just jealous. She doesn't want anyone to go near Mary, or for Elaine to take up with someone else. You happened to be the one to borrow Mary's car and make the introduction. Nichole isn't mad at you. She's mad that there's so many gays in town, and she's mad that her father disapproves of her when he did the same damn thing 20 years ago. You just happened to get between her and both those grievances. And Mary's not mad at you. If she wanted to see her mother, she would have found a way. She probably didn't want to see her die. You said yourself you watched your mother die, and you've regretted it ever since. I think you care about your mistakes more than anyone, but in a vain way, as if you've overestimated your importance. If you *really* cared, or thought what you did was so bad, you wouldn't do it. You just wouldn't do it."

I hadn't watched my mother die. That's what I regretted ever since. I couldn't remember anything about my mother, except that she was Swedish, looked like Ingrid Bergman, had worked for the FBI, had smoked, and died of lung cancer. And I certainly did not remember seeing my mother die. I distinctly remembered not ever having been there.

Gabe had put his hand on my arm. "Kate, Kate. Did I hurt your feelings?"

I looked at him. It was as if I had left the room for a few minutes and had come back.

"No," I said.

"You always space out when you can't handle something. Hey, maybe that's what the amnesia is about."

He sounded hopeful. "Maybe," I said.

"I thought you slept around because you didn't want me to find out you were ordinary. That's not really love, you know, that's desire. So what do you think of these sketches?"

He lifted up one of the sheets, and let it fall back against the wall.

"I was wondering why you took it up again, when just last night you were happy you'd dropped it."

Gabe sat down on the floor and leafed through the magazines, as if he were reviewing their contents. "I don't know," he said. "I went into Ethan's Pharmacy this morning, and I saw Harper on the cover of all those magazines, and I thought sure, part of what he's doing is hype, a big part, I mean, I think he planned the whole arrest just for the publicity, but he's really done something, he's really influenced public opinion, and made an audience for himself, and—" He put the magazines down. "I don't know. It gave me a sense of efficacy, I guess. A sense of hope." He got up, stalked around the room, then approached the wall and inspected his sketches again. "Anyway, I just enjoy doing it—graphic design, I mean. I denied that for a long time."

"So you might take it up again?"

"I might." He went over to the video machine and turned it off. He climbed the stairs to the loft, and then turned to see if I were coming. When he looked at me his face changed suddenly, as if he just remembered something. I followed him up.

***

In the morning, when I woke up, Gabe was looking at me, and he wore that same expression of fear on his face. He sat up in bed and laid his cool palm against my forehead as if I were his patient. "Will you try some tests," he said, "to try and get your memory back?"

"I've been all through that," I said, "at the Clinic."

"I don't mean at the Clinic. I don't even mean doctors necessarily."

"Then what do you mean?"

"When someone's cancer is incurable they go to Mexico and get laetrile, or try macrobiotic food. You know. There's got to be something like that we could try. Something the doctors don't approve of. I don't have anything in mind yet, but if I look into it, and find out something, will you try it?"

"Depends on what it is."

"I'll let you know then." He took his hand off my forehead, and got up out of bed. The fear in his expression cleared suddenly, and he started laughing. "I could make up stories," he said.

I smiled at him. I was glad that he was starting to feel better.

Chapter Four

Thursday

When I arrived at the law office Thursday morning, a crowd had gathered outside. The onlookers stood motionless, as if they had stopped to gape at an accident. Only the TV crews ran around stringing wires, carrying lights and cameras, but even they seemed stunned—in the frantic way they were angling for shots they appeared more anxious than persistent.

Getz had positioned himself in front of the door, and stood there as if transfixed, with his legs spread at shoulder width and his arms crossed against his chest, like a wooden Indian in front of a dry goods store, like a warning not to approach. He stood aside to let me pass and, when I did, he whispered: "The collaborators weren't indicted." Then he winked at me.

Inside the office Julie answered the telephone, asking each person to hold, until all the phone buttons were blinking.

Presently someone would hang up and free the line for another person to get through, and she would have to answer again and ask the new person to hold, so that all the phone buttons would remain blinking. It was like a child's game. Ruth rushed through the office hurling files into a box and briefcase, and pulling at her skirt and necklace, while issuing commands into a hand-held tape recorder. She kept glancing at her watch, then the clock on the wall, then the telephone, then the copy machine, then the enormous tail of a tuna that was mounted above the file cabinets. She had caught the tuna on a fishing trip with Angelo. Angelo was upstairs yelling questions down about which nylons, handkerchiefs and jewelry he should pack, and finally emerged carrying a suitcase.

Ruth turned to watch Angelo descend the stairs and noticed that I was standing in the room, wondering what to do. "Thank God you're here," Ruth said. "I should take you with me."

"You can't take her," Angelo said. "You need her here."

"What's going on?" I said.

Ruth flipped the tape out of the pocket-sized recorder, and folded my hand over it, as if it were hush money.

"Harper's been indicted on U.S. Trade violations," she said. "His art dealer hired some hot-shot New York lawyer and they want me there as a consultant during the pre-trial arbitration. They're hoping to settle before it goes to trial."

"It won't go to trial," Angelo said.

The phone rang again and Julie put the caller on hold. Angelo dragged the suitcase to the door and knocked to signal that they were ready to leave. Getz raised his hand and pulled on his earring to indicate that he understood. "All your instructions are on the tape," Ruth said. "What to tell the investors, what to tell the press if they corner you. Getz is going to stay by the door after we leave until the crowd thins out."

"Do you have everything?" I said.

"I think so." She picked up her box and briefcase. "I may call you to express some documents to me, if I've forgotten anything."

"Enough of these long goodbyes," Angelo said. "She'll manage."

I didn't know what to say. They were like desperadoes; Ruth and Angelo could have been Bonnie and Clyde, or Butch Cassidy and the Sundance Kid, and the crowd outside the 157th Cavalry, ready to gun them down. Ruth patted my hand—the one that held the tape. "Listen to that first," she said, and they ran out the door, ducking under microphones and spotlights to the Cadillac Seville. Julie and I watched from the window until they drove away. Then the phone began to ring again.

"You sure know when to show up," Julie said. "You should have been here when she found out she had to be on the plane in an hour. She drove us all crazy trying to pack and get her ready. I made the plane reservation."

Julie rolled her eyes and tried to put the caller on hold, but it was her father, Jack Souza, from Provincetown National Bank, so she told him what was happening.

Getz came inside, locked the door and shut the curtains. "Isn't this fun?" he said.

"When did they indict him?" I said.

"Early this morning," he said. He looked out the window briefly, and then turned to me and studied my face. "Don't worry. It won't even go to trial. They'll settle out of court. He'll get fined or something, not even a jail sentence. They don't want more publicity for this thing. Really." He checked out the window again.

"Is he in jail now?" I said. I turned the tape over in my hand.

"The lawyer got him out on bail." He checked another window. "They're giving up. They're starting to get bored and go away."

"Is this lawyer any good? Will he be able to get him released?"

Getz went over to me and took hold of my arm. "Hey," he said, "stop worrying, okay? The Feds don't want any more publicity from this than they have to. He won't get a jail term." He stopped and looked at me. "What are you, in love with this guy?" He tugged on my arm like a child who wants his mother to buy him a toy. "Well anyway, they're not going to indict any of the collaborators. Harper is taking the full rap on himself." He winked again.

Julie hung up the phone. "You always show after the heat is off," she went on. "You should have seen this place, people shoving microphones in the windows, Ruth running around trying to find the right files. Every time she asked me for something I kept telling her, Kate knows where that is, Kate knows where that is, and she kept yelling: 'Where's Kate? Why isn't Kate here?' I thought you went to see Josh at the Karate show or something."

"I decided to do some work for a change," I said.

"Well, it's all over now," she said. "Oh, and Dad says if you need any documents, just phone him."

"Thanks," I said. I looked at the tape in my hand.

"Can I unplug the phone now?" she said.

"What the hell," Getz said.

She did. The phone upstairs started ringing. "That's the home number," she said.

"We better check it," he said, and winked at me. He took me by the hand and started upstairs.

"Is Angelo coming back?" I whispered. I felt like I was in high school, and had been asked to make love when her boyfriend's parents were in the next room.

"He won't stop here. He'll go straight home."

"Hey!" Julie yelled. We stopped on the stairs. "Shouldn't you listen to the tape first?" She smiled at us like an accomplice, her face full of treachery and cunning.

We spent the day in bed; in the evening Getz turned the news on. "Do you think they'll show the house?" he said. He wanted to see himself on television.

When Julie heard the noise of the television, she yelled up the stairs that she was going home for the day, and reminded me to listen to the tape before I left. I said I would. Then Julie said she was sending the baby Puma up.

"Puma's here?" I said.

"Been here all day," Getz said. "She was installed on a window ledge when all the fuss was going on, and has been playing downstairs since. She amuses herself."

The baby Puma waddled in to the bedroom carrying an empty honey jar. She climbed on the bed and into my lap. "Do you sleep naked?" she asked me. "Sometimes my daddy sleeps naked." She sounded apologetic, the way an aunt might excuse her nephew's embarrassing stutter or tick.

"That's glass," Getz said gently, resting his fingertips on the honey jar. "You need to be careful with it or it will break."

Puma turned the jar over in her hands and gazed at it in wonderment as if it had transformed. On the television Dan Rather said that Harper Martin had been indicted on U.S. Trade violations, but no others had been indicted. An inset photograph of the defense attorney chosen for the case appeared on the screen. Dan Rather said that he was a former United States Attorney.

Dan Rather said that the defense team had summoned Harper Martin's Provincetown attorney, Ruth Allen Esq., to serve as a consultant in the pre-trial arbitration. The screen showed film clips of Angelo ushering Ruth to the car, and Getz could be seen in the background, guarding the office door. "You look like a mass murderer in that shot," I said.

"Home movies, Daddy!" the baby Puma said, and crawled down my leg to sit on my feet, closer to the television. Dan Rather said that both sides hoped to settle the case in pre-trial arbitration, and that the demonstrations for Harper Martin and against United States intervention in South America were growing. They showed film clips of more demonstrations, the slogans on the signs were the same: *No Vietnam War in South America* and *Free Harper Martin*. "Home movies, Daddy," the baby Puma repeated, waving the honey jar at him, and then looking through it as if it were a telescope. "Home movies."

Getz reached across the bed and took the jar out of her hand. "That's right," he said. "Home movies."

***

The tape Ruth had made directed me to pay a visit to each of the investors of Maniac Drifter Inc., and inform them in person that Harper had been formally indicted, none of the collaborators had been indicted, and Ruth had gone to New York to assist the defense attorney with the pre-trial arbitration proceedings. Of course, the investors would have already heard the news, but it was a politeness and a courtesy, as the attorney for Maniac Drifter Inc., for Ruth to personally deliver the news, and since Ruth would be out of town, it was my job to do it. The tape also instructed me to tell the investors that Ruth would, as the corporate attorney in the case, do everything in her power to preserve the stockholders' investments.

At the Bad Attitude Café and Cinema, I found Antaeus in his office, flipping restlessly through a pile of receipts. He turned now and then to make an entry in the account book on his right, but paused each time, as if he were trying to decide whether to falsify it or not. When he saw me he jumped up and greeted me like an old friend, patting me on the back and shaking my hand simultaneously. Perhaps he considered my arrival propitious, since it saved him from committing a felony.

"Kate, Kate, welcome," he said, pumping my hand more times than was acceptable.

I wondered why people often said my name twice, as if the monosyllable was not substantial or someone had forced them to recall me after a long absence: Yes, Kate, Kate. I remember her well.

"Did you come to see the new gallery?" he asked, looking up at the ceiling.

"Actually, I came with a message from Ruth."

"From Ruth!" Antaeus said, giggling as if he were embarrassed. "So what did Ruth want to tell me?"

I launched into my speech about how Harper had been indicted for U.S. Trade violations but none of the collaborators had been indicted, Ruth had left for New York to work as a consultant to the defense attorney, that they hoped to settle in pre-trial arbitration, and Ruth would do everything in her power to preserve the stockholders' investments.

When I reached the part about the stockholders' investments, Antaeus started laughing uproariously, his reckless, violent, uncontrolled laugh. "I know," I said, "you've heard this all on television already but—"

He put out his hand, as if to stop a car that was approaching. "No," he said, still laughing, but more calmly now. "It's not that. Don't you know what's going on?"

"What's going on?"

"Don't you know how much money we're making off this thing?" he whispered and looked around.

I looked, too.

"Well with all the publicity from the Temple of the Jaguars story, and Benefit Week, and everyone in town—"

He started chuckling to himself and beat his fist quietly against the wall like a drum beat. It reminded me of the investors meeting—he beat on the pool table when he finally got the joke. I didn't get it yet.

"So you don't know," he said.

I shook my head. Antaeus shut the door to his office. "He gets royalties," he said. He looked at my blank expression and tried again. "Don't you understand? He gets a percentage of the profits from the thing, like royalties."

"Profits from the exhibit?"

Antaeus nodded. "For the first 50 years. He convinced them he should be paid for the publicity he would cause—he used his painting the murals as an example. He told them a flat rate for the artifacts and his work painting the mural wouldn't be a fair assessment of his contribution if the thing really became popular. So he'll receive royalties, the way an actor will take the percentage of the profits on a movie, instead of being paid a flat fee to act in it."

"Jesus, can he do that?"

"He did it. And the Getty Museum's attendance has tripled in the last three weeks since the story broke. The Temple of the Jaguars exhibit hasn't even opened yet! Think of when he gets out of jail and he's painting that mural. Imagine how many people are going to show up there!" He let loose another great laugh, larger than himself, as if the universe had played a joke on him, and by a stroke of luck he had profited by it.

"So the investors get part of that money?"

"We're the stockholders in the company," he explained. "And our stock just keeps going up." He chuckled to himself again, and fluffed the stack of receipts on his desk, as if, now that he remembered his impending wealth, they meant nothing to him.

"What if Harper gets thrown in jail, or they have to give the artifacts back, or they won't give the confiscated crates back or—?"

Antaeus waved his hands to stop me. "The government can't afford the backlash. Public opinion is against them now. There would be demonstrations in the street. It would be like the Sixties again. And the funny thing about it is, do you think Harper cares about Nicaragua? I don't think so. I don't think he even considered the moral issues of the war there, or our part in it. But my god, look how he's used it in his favor, to get public opinion on his side so he can have what he wants. They can't lock him up, they can't take the artifacts away from him. The public would be outraged. Harper's made himself into a hero. A real American outlaw hero." Antaeus shook his head. "I just thought I was investing a little money so some artist in town could get an even break. I didn't know what I was doing. This guy is a genius. He's a gold mine. He's absolutely incorrigible."

He sat down at his desk and held his head in his hands. He looked devastated.

"So what's the matter?" I said.

"What's the matter?" He took his hands away and looked up at me. He shrugged. "What's the matter?" He looked around vacantly, as if he were in shock, or had been unfrozen after 200 years and had no idea what the world was like anymore. "It's bigger than all of us. It's out of control. Look what's happening here in town. Everyone's building, real estate prices are going up, everyone's renovating, different kinds of people are coming here, people with more money."

"Gentrification," I said.

"Exactly. In a few years no one will remember Harper Martin, but the whole town will be different. Some of us locals will have made it through the change alright, sure, but the fishermen and the Portuguese and the old townies won't be able to afford to live here anymore." I nodded. "Say every year you take a vacation in Vegas, and you've been playing at the five dollar black jack table all your life. Then one day, some guy named Harper Martin walks in, and moves you over to the twenty-five dollar blackjack table without you even realizing it. You play well there, it's not that, but you've never played at this table. It's bigger than you. You feel you don't belong there. Do you understand?"

I nodded. "I think so," I said. I looked at my watch and said I had to go.

"Raphael next?"

I said yes and wondered if he were thinking of the hit and run accident in which his mother killed Raphael's mother.

"Raphael understood what Harper was doing," he said. "Right from the very beginning."

I nodded, remembering Raphael's contented, Buddha-like composure at the Beachcombers investors meeting. Antaeus stood up and shook my hand.

"I never thanked you for helping with the liquor license appeal for the gallery," he said. "I appreciate it."

"It was nothing."

"Well, there will be liquor served from the new bar at Cosmo's opening. And I insist on serving you personally, by way of thanks. Don't try to slip by me in the crowd."

"It was really nothing. I just notified the abutters."

"I can't stand a person who won't accept gratitude," he said, and waved me out the door, as if he were fanning air.

***

It was not only women who came to see Paula and Christianne's cabaret performance to benefit the Harper Martin Defense Fund. Most of the crowd at Paradiso's on Thursday night were locals who came to demonstrate their support for the Benefit, pay tribute to the performers, and signal the importance of the occasion with their presence, the way they would come on the opening and closing nights of the season.

When I arrived, Joe Houston was leaning against the bar, talking to Mary. He had changed out of his Mayan Ballplayer's costume, and was wearing his regulation black jeans, black t-shirt with *Bad Attitude* written in magenta script across the chest, a pack of Gauloises rolled up in his sleeve, and of course, the black take-up-reel glove. Raphael Souza sat at a back table talking to Antaeus, as if to show publicly that he bore no grudge against him over Mrs. Souza's death, and in bearing none, upheld his status as Town Martyr. Elaine and Whitney sat at the table opposite center stage, where Whitney had sat the first night she met Elaine. Whitney was wearing the same tiger shirt and tiger-striped socks that had attracted Montana Devon's attention that night, and caused Elaine to notice her. They sat leaning against each other with a smug satisfaction, almost contemptuous of the idea that they could have ever been apart, anticipating Montana's surprise when he would see them together and realize they had taken his advice. On the table in front of them their beer bottles touched. Elaine lit a Player's and after she blew out the first drag of smoke, whispered something in Whitney's ear.

The night that Whitney met Elaine, I hadn't planned to take Whitney to Paradiso's. It just happened. We were sitting on the steps of Animus Pizza. I was drinking my chocolate egg cream. The front door to Paradiso's was just across the street and down the alley. Christianne, the French-Canadian singer who performed there, was standing at the door in her tuxedo, leaning on a cane. Her chestnut hair was cut short to show off her high cheekbones and green eyes. When she sang her voice was powerful and sad, as if she'd dredged up some solitary, private grief. Before a performance she would linger at the doorway like that, all sad and dreamy, looking up at the stars.

Whitney had been complaining about the men she was trying to see, so I suggested she might try women, and pointed down the alley. Whitney asked me if I liked cross-dressing and said that androgyny was just a fad. I told her that Christianne was no fad, and asked if she'd ever heard her sing. Whitney said she hadn't. It was my night off from Cosmo's restaurant, so we decided to go. Whitney asked me if we should go get Nichole, but I told her Nichole got upset about the gay scene and wouldn't want to. I threw away my chocolate egg cream and we got up. That's when I noticed Whitney's tiger-striped knee socks for the first time. They went with her growling tiger shirt.

While I was inspecting the socks Lydia Street rode up on her bicycle. She was wearing her khaki safari shorts, a Hawaiian flowered shirt, a denim railroad cap and tennis shoes. She had strawberry blond hair, green eyes and freckles. Her bike was a royal blue, decorated with red plastic poinsettias and green plastic leaves. Both the poinsettias and leaves could be popped off the vines at their joints and snapped back in again. In the front basket of the bike she carried her pet parrot Sydney Greenstreet, in a wicker birdcage. Lydia wrote the weekly gossip column for the *Provincetown Express* and played in the annual tennis tournament. The previous winter she had taken a trip to Africa where, she claimed, a lion chased her into her tent.

Whitney and I walked down the alley to Paradiso's. The show was not scheduled to start for a half an hour but a line had already formed at the door. The women liked to arrive early so they could select the best seats. Inside, the dance floor was filled with tables and chairs. Whitney chose one center stage. I asked her if she wanted to sit in the back where she could get the full effect, but she said she preferred the front row. I went to Mary at the bar and got Whitney a Heineken and myself a club soda. Falzano was leaning on the counter at the waitress station, wearing a black silk bowling shirt with beige, red and yellow rectangles on it like a Mondrian painting. She wore a gold chain around her wrist and she smelled like Pierre Cardin. Falzano didn't remember me so Mary introduced me as Ruth Allen Esquire's assistant. Then Falzano noticed I was drinking club soda and raised the price because it was show time. When Mary tried to explain I didn't drink, Falzano said that nobody drank. She runs a nightclub in the sleaziest town in the country and nobody drinks. She asked us if we thought she could make money from the nightly cover charge. She told us not to be ridiculous. A nightclub made money from liquor. And nobody drank. So club soda cost a dollar fifty during show times. It was a new rule. Mary was to tell the waitresses.

Falzano left and Mary wouldn't take my money, so I put it in the tip jar. I apologized for getting her in trouble but she said she wasn't in trouble; Falzano just got nervous before the show started. Then we arranged a meeting place and time because that was the night I was driving her to Boston to see her mom.

Falzano came back to the bar with Christianne. Christianne had her tuxedo on for the show and was smoking a Gitanes. She smelled like men's Givenchy. She asked Mary for a scotch and soda and asked who the beautiful girl was. She stole a glance at me, looked away, and took a drag on her cigarette. Falzano said I was Ruth's assistant. Mary introduced me as Kate. Christianne said she was enchanted and kissed my hand. Falzano complained that I didn't drink. Christianne said well of course not, she's so sweet and pure. Then she told me not to let Falzano upset me, and patted the hand she had kissed. Falzano asked where Paula was and Christianne said she was putting on her makeup. She rolled her eyes and pointed upstairs at the dressing room. She took her scotch from Mary and twirled the swizzle stick around in it, rattling the ice. She asked me if I was here for the show. When I said I was she said she was happy now. She picked up her scotch and Gitanes, said goodbye darling to me, I miss you already, and left. Mary laughed and called her a ham.

When I got back to the table the room was full of people and Whitney already had a Heineken. I asked her where she got it and she pointed to Slashette, the cocktail waitress with the stingray haircut. It was shaved close to the head on the left side and was long on the right. It was dyed blond, but the roots showed underneath. It was not fashionable to pretend your hair color was real. Slashette wrote the Fashion Espionage column for the *Provincetown Express* and appeared in a photo above the copy in a trench coat, fedora and sunglasses.

Whitney told me Slashette wanted to be a fashion model. Then she pointed to Elaine Barry, who was sitting to the right of the stage and asked who that thin, pretty, forty-ish woman with the exquisite silver hair might be. I told her she was Raphael Souza's sister, she worked at Ethan's

Pharmacy, she was a friend of Mary's and she was gay. Whitney said she looked like Lauren Bacall but didn't believe she was gay. I said she was also divorced and had two kids in college. Whitney pointed out Lydia and called her the Bike Lady. Lydia had stationed Sydney Greenstreet on the bar counter and was straddling one of the high stools in the back.

The lights went down and the women started clapping, cheering and screaming. Christianne emerged from behind the curtain and the screaming got louder. A few women tossed roses onto the stage. "Girls, girls," Christianne said into the microphone and held up her hands. She asked everyone to stay calm and told them she would sing to them later, but first, she wanted to introduce her good friend Montana Devon.

Everyone clapped. A very tall, gorgeous woman in a skin-tight silver-lamé dress walked out onto the stage. The dress was slit almost all the way up her thighs on both sides, showing off her long, slender, curvaceous legs. Her red hair was swept up in a French twist, and the color matched her long red fingernails. She gave Christianne a kiss on the forehead. Christianne pretended to swoon, then blushed, bowed, and left the stage.

Montana took the microphone off its stand. She said hello and waved at the audience. The women said hello. Montana said she couldn't believe how many girls they had in the audience that night and patted the back of her French twist in a mock primping gesture. Then she set her hand on her hip and asked if anyone had been to any Tupperware parties lately. Her voice resembled Mae West's, rude and vampy.

Whitney leaned toward me and scolded me for not telling her there was a warm-up act. She asked me if Montana was strictly a comedian or if she might sing. I told her Montana was a guy. Whitney said, No way. I said, Swear to god.

Montana asked the crowd if they liked her dress. The women hooted, clapped and cheered. Montana ran her hand up and down her silver-lamé thigh. She said the dress was beaded by 423 Portuguese lesbians. Then she asked the technicians to turn the spotlight off and the house lights up. She wanted to see all the beautiful girls. She called to Lydia in the back of the room and asked if Sydney Greenstreet was with her. Lydia coaxed the parrot off the bar counter and onto her hand. She held him up so Montana could see him. The crowd clapped. Montana asked if Sydney was enjoying the show. Lydia whispered something to Sydney and the parrot squawked, "Stunning! Stunning!"

Montana thanked Sydney and told Lydia she wanted to ask her a personal question. She said she didn't have to answer in front of all those people, but Montana hoped she would tell her in private after the show. She said the question was about Sydney. She said Lydia and Sydney had been together for a long time now and people said it was the only ongoing monogamous relationship in town. But Montana said she was worried. She'd seen Sydney Greenstreet at the White Sands a few times and he wore those funny carves and his cage was all decorated with poinsettias, and she didn't know how to break it to Lydia, but did she think maybe Sydney Greenstreet was gay?

Montana circulated among the front tables, taunting the people she knew. She made a few jokes about Falzano, Mary and Slashette. Then she spotted Elaine Barry's hair.

She approached Elaine and touched her hair. She remarked on what a beautiful color it was and asked the crowd what they thought. The women clapped. She asked Elaine if it were real. Elaine shook her head. Montana wanted to know if it were Sassoon or Cardin or Yves Saint Laurent. Elaine said it was Clairol. Montana gave the crowd a knowing look. That's when she spotted Whitney. She lifted a shock of Whitney's hair and displayed it to the audience. She asked them if it wasn't exquisite and asked them what color it was, perhaps fuchsia. She stepped back, appraising the hair. She asked the crowd if she should dye her hair that color. The crowd hooted. She said she would. Then she said that Elaine and Whitney should get together. The crowd applauded and shouted things like, *Right On!* and, *Go for it!*

Then Montana stepped back and pointed at Whitney's ankles. She made her put her leg up on the table. She had them shine the spotlight on Whitney's ankles. She had forgotten to roll her jeans back down and her tiger-striped knee socks were showing. Montana asked the audience if Whitney were a hot number or what. She asked them to look at the tiger legs. She said that Whitney was hotter than Tina Turner in *Mad Max Beyond Thunderdome*. The crowd howled. Whitney put her head down and buried her face in the table. When she looked up again, the spotlight had been turned off and Elaine Barry was smiling sympathetically at her.

Montana harassed a few more people in the audience, told Lydia Street she liked her Flintstones hairdo and then introduced Christianne and Paula. Whitney whispered to me she was embarrassed and I whispered back that she had picked the front row table.

Christianne and Paula had been standing on the sidelines watching Montana. They both chain-smoked. Christianne kept throwing her shoulders back, jutting her chin out and clearing her throat, as if someone had told her to stand up straight. Paula practiced some scales and tried to get Christianne to join her but she just leaned her head on Paula's shoulder and said, I want to go home! Then she took one last sip of her scotch; they extinguished their cigarettes, and went up on stage.

They sang a medley of "Them Their Eyes" and "Dream a Little Dream of Me"; then Christianne stepped aside while Paula sang "The Man Who Got Away." Whitney told me she thought Paula was much more attractive than Christianne, more genuine and down to earth. A lot of women thought so. If many had become outspoken, moony insomniacs over Christianne, an equal population harbored a private, undeclared crush on Paula. After all, she owned the bar with Falzano; she had been stolen away from Falzano; she was the mother of twin daughters, a New Yorker who had understudied to Barbara Streisand on Broadway. She was nervous, vulnerable and feminine, smoked cigarettes on long, ivory holders. Some of the locals thought the women's community in Provincetown could be divided into those who had a crush on Christianne and those who had a weakness for Paula.

When "The Man Who Got Away" was over, Paula left the stage looking relieved. The applause and hooting were deafening but you could still hear Christianne's voice above it.

Christianne positioned herself at center stage and sang "Teach Me Tonight." The crowd was silent when she started. She was very serious; all the teasing had gone. She glanced at the music on the podium and treated the English words gingerly. Her diffidence was charming. After a while she seemed to be drawn into the music, and brought it out in the strongest, sexiest, romantic French voice, an Edith Piaf without the waifishness. The crowd started screaming as if she were Frank Sinatra.

When she finished I leaned over to Whitney and asked if she believed me now. Whitney nodded and said she got the picture. The performers left the stage; the house lights came up. Everyone looked dazed, as if their houses had burned down and their lovers had left them. Friends avoided each other's gaze. Except for Whitney and Elaine. They looked at each other for quite awhile, and then smiled and looked down.

The next day Whitney and Elaine were seen having coffee at the Bad Attitude Café. After that they had dinner in Cosmo's restaurant. Pretty soon they were a couple and invited me over for paella at Raphael's house. That's the whole story.

But tonight at Paradiso's it was a different scene entirely. Whitney and Elaine were together. Cosmo wandered through the room greeting people at different tables, as if he owned the establishment and wanted to make sure everyone was comfortable. At the same time he kept scanning the tables and entrances, as if he were expecting someone in particular, and wanted to be prepared when they came in. Falzano patrolled the room in a bowling shirt and pants, giving orders to the cocktail waitresses and jabbing friends in the ribs as she walked by their tables. The talk around the bar concerned Harper's indictment: the hot-shot New York attorney, Ruth's departure to work as a consultant on the case, whether or not the Benefit Fund would cover the legal fees if the case went to trial, and the fact that none of the collaborators had been indicted.

Lydia Street stood in the back of the room talking to Edward the real estate agent and petting his blind collie. Edward held one end of the collie's leash in his hand, and the dog chewed the other end. Lydia was wearing a black trench coat and sunglasses. She had made tiny cardboard sunglasses for Sydney Greenstreet, but they fell off every time the parrot moved his head. Sydney squawked: "That takes the proverbial biscuit!" at the collie, and the dog barked back, causing the leash to fall out of its mouth. When the two animals were finished, Edward bent down and reinserted the leash into the dog's mouth.

When Cosmo noticed me, he took in a deep breath and looked beyond me, as if he expected someone to be following behind. When no one else appeared, Cosmo sighed, shook his head and continued to wander aimlessly around the bar. Elaine and Whitney waved to me; Whitney pointed at the table, and then at her tiger-striped knee socks, to remind me of their significance. I stood in the corner by the piano and watched Joe talk to Mary at the bar. Mary looked the same—tough and restrained. I marveled at the way the experiences of loss and death were not revealed in some people's manner or expressions. Joe was talking fast and gesticulating wildly, then he leaned in closer to Mary and began to talk more softly, as if he were trying to convince her of something, or disclose a confidence. Mary laughed and looked up; she smiled when she saw me. Joe turned around and motioned me over to the bar.

"I was right," he said to me. "Fashion Espionage was really great. You shouldn't have left."

"What are you drinking, honey?" Mary said, and smiled reassuringly. "It's on me."

"I don't need anything," I said.

"I'm sorry," Joe said. "I should have offered myself. What am I thinking about?"

"The Fashion Espionage show," Mary said, and began fixing a club soda with lime. "Tell her what happened."

"Slashette did an imitation of Paula singing 'One of the Boys,' and when the spies finally took off their trench coats they were wearing these little holsters with guns in them instead of G-strings."

"Cute," Mary said. She slid my drink across the bar counter. I tried to pay but Mary ignored the money so Joe stuffed it in the tip jar.

"Some truck driver from Brockton won the djellaba. And then, when everybody thought it was over, they opened the curtains on stage, there was a screen behind, and they showed a video of the Pierre Cardin Pre-Columbian Fall Fashion Preview. It opened in Paris yesterday. Can you believe this?

"The costumes were amazing," Joe went on. "The headdresses had feathers and jewels sewn into them; the snake belts came with Aztec suns on the buckles; and fur capes had hieroglyph designs branded around the edges, you know—like a Miro painting, and hoods designed as jaguar heads with open mouths. There were lots of bare legs and midriffs, lots of *skin*, as Lance would say. Now that I think about it, the costumes seemed more Egyptian than Pre-Columbian to me."

"It's not costumes, it's haute couture," Mary said. "Haute couture. People are going to wear those outfits to the symphony."

"Oh my god," he said. "I never thought of that." He took a sip of his beer. "Anyway, then CBS asked the Mother of the Year to parade down the gangplank a second time in her Goddess of Sin costume, and filmed the whole thing, right down to the squid necklace."

"What will CBS do with this film?" I said.

"Maybe they'll use it in a special segment of *Sixty Minutes*," Mary said, chuckling to herself.

"Aren't they doing a special report on Benefit Week?" I said. "Maybe that's what it's for." I looked around for the television crews. "No cameramen here?"

Mary pointed above their heads. "On the balcony," she said. "Falzano didn't want them disturbing the customers."

Joe took the pack of Gauloises out of his shirtsleeve and lit one. He watched Mary regard me, and then began to fidget and look around the room. "Well, I think Elaine is calling for me," he said, and left the bar. Mary and I watched him saunter over to Elaine and Whitney's table, pull two magazines out of his back pocket and spread them flat on the table in front of them, holding the edges down with their beer bottles.

"Harper's on the cover of *Time* and *Newsweek*," Mary explained. "They were sold out at Ethan's Pharmacy by noon."

"I saw," I said. I shifted my weight from one leg to the other, and then back again, unable to get comfortable, and twirled the straw around in the glass of club soda.

Mary filled the drink orders for Slashette and Trudy, Paula's daughter, who also worked as a cocktail waitress on busy nights. "You weren't at the Karate show this morning," Mary said. "Joshua was asking for you. He seemed disappointed you didn't come."

"I was at the law office."

Mary nodded and gave me a wry smile. "Why don't you come around here and rub my back?"

"I can go behind the bar?"

"Of course."

"Falzano won't mind?"

Mary laughed at me. "So," she said as I rubbed her back, "I heard you made a fuss about bringing the car back after I'd left."

"Made a fuss? But—"

"No buts. I told you to bring the car back by Tuesday. You didn't. Maybe you had a rough week. Anyway, I forgive you. So just get over it."

"But—" Even though Mary did not interrupt me, I didn't finish. I did not understand how Mary forgave me, or Raphael forgave Antaeus or Nello forgave Cosmo or the owner of the Zanzibar forgave Getz. And yet they did. They did.

It had happened this way. After our trip to Boston, Mary told me I could borrow her car while I got mine fixed. So I did. I didn't return it on time. While I was late her mother had a cerebral hemorrhage and went into a coma. She was gone in three hours. Mary went up the next morning. She flew up. I still hadn't returned the car. But if I had brought the car back when I was supposed to, Mary would have seen her mother before she died.

Elaine and Whitney were at Mary's when I returned the car, to break the news. They knew I'd blame myself. Whitney said it wasn't my fault. Elaine said Mary couldn't have gotten there any faster in a car. I said I could have sped and gotten her there in time. I asked her where the hospital was. I was calculating the speed I would have had to drive.

Whitney said she could have borrowed a car but I couldn't think of one she could have borrowed. Whitney said nobody was blaming me. Falzano and Raphael had cars she could have borrowed. I said if I had brought the car back when I said I would she could have gotten there in time to see her mother alive. That was the bottom line. Whitney said maybe Mary didn't want to see her mother in a coma. She said maybe I did her a favor. I said I had let her down. Elaine insisted it wasn't my fault. The night my mother died I had refused to go to the hospital. I was terrified to see a person die. My mother told me I didn't have to go. She knew she wouldn't be able to breathe on her own. I took my mother's advice and didn't go. I had always regretted it. I was a coward.

"You have to forgive yourself," Mary was saying, at the bar at Paradiso's.

"I can't."

"I know. But that's the problem. And I'm sorry about Grace."

"This is absurd. You don't have to—"

"I told Grace she was completely out of line yelling at you like that. I don't care what she learned in AA. I told her not to come tonight."

I had stopped massaging Mary's shoulders. I didn't say anything. I wanted to say, *If I had brought the car back in time you would have been able to see your mother alive*, but I was afraid to say it. I knew it was not Mary's way to address things directly.

"Are you pouting?" she said.

"You sound mad."

"I am mad, but not at you."

I began to rub her back again. “So what about you?” I said. “How are you doing?”

“I’m doing okay. I’m okay.” Then: “I’m worried about him. I may have to go up there for the winter and keep him company. But that would be alright.”

She got up to make more drinks. The room was full now, there were people standing up in the back. Falzano was cueing the lights.

“Better sit down,” she said. “They’re going to start.”

“Mary. I’m sorry about your mom.”

Mary ran a glass through the ice bucket and looked up. “I know you are.”

The lights went out, Montana Devon came on stage and announced that Harper Martin had been indicted for U.S. trade violations. Then he noticed Elaine and Whitney, sitting right in front of him with their arms around each other, and began to squeal in his falsetto.

***

Friday

When I woke up Friday morning I had no idea where I was. The bedroom seemed nice enough; it smelled of newly sawed wood and fresh paint. I was alone in a big bed, underneath a thick quilted coverlet. A hope chest stood at the foot of the bed. The closet door was open, and a dozen pairs of running shoes sat in neat rows on the floor inside, like couples waiting to dance. I read the inscription on the t-shirt I was wearing, it said, *14th MARLBORO INVITATIONAL*. Why am I doing this? I thought.

In another room a food processor whizzed and a stern voice came from a television set. Then a real voice yelled, "I made you a protein shake!" I got out of bed and walked down the hallway toward the voice.

Mary was standing in the kitchen holding a glass of brown liquid out to me. "I put papayas, kiwis and protein powder in it," she said. "Go ahead."

I sat down dumbstruck at the table and stared in stupefaction at the television set. Mary? I thought. *Mary*?

The trip to Boston had been entirely innocent. When Mary finished work at Paradiso's, I got in her car on the driver's side and she gave me a set of keys. Mary let her seatback down and curled up on it. I started the car, fastened the seat belt, turned the defroster on, adjusted the mirrors, inspected the dials, and gauges. I felt comfortable in a car. This was my territory. After all, I had grown up in Los Angeles. Behind the wheel I was in control.

Mary asked me why she had to work so much when her mom was sick. She worked every night at Paradiso's and every day at the video rental counter at Ethan's Pharmacy so she was too tired to drive herself to her parents' house. That was why she was allowing me to drive her. Even so I had to insist; Mary was one of those people who was always helping others, but would not take any help from anyone unless they forced it on her.

Mary's mom had been dying of a brain tumor. She lived with Mary's dad in a suburb of Boston, where Mary grew up. Mary's father had been a bartender, until he retired. Both parents were in their seventies. Mary was around 40, the age my mother had been when she died. Mary was quiet, tough and restrained, but sweet and tormented, like

James Dean in *Rebel Without a Cause*. She had a plastic hip, so she walked with a limp sometimes, but that was much better than her childhood, which she spent part in a wheelchair, part in a cast, part on crutches. They did not have plastic hips then and they did not know what to do for her. Now she played basketball, and went running every day in her Marlboro t-shirt. She got involved with the cute young girls, "tinker dykes" as Grace called them, and took care of them through the winter. When summer came they left her to model, or lift weights or join the karate championships or whatever they left her for. Mary always got another one; she was the most popular bartender in town. I said it was her James Dean appeal—tough, tender and restrained.

Mary was asking me what was happening with me. People were always asking after each other's news. The event was not really important; it was the exchange of information that mattered. I told her I was worried about Harper and she asked me if he had fallen off the wagon. Almost everyone in town was either in Alcoholics Anonymous or Friends of Alcoholics Anonymous. Different groups met together on different nights. The lesbians met Thursday nights. The painters met Wednesday. If your girlfriend or boyfriend was in Alcoholics Anonymous, you had to be in Friends of.

Mary said whatever was happening with Harper I should just let it happen. It would come to me. I couldn't help him if he didn't want me to. That was Alcoholics Anonymous talk. Mary was in Friends of. I knew the jargon. I never quarreled with Mary or anyone else when they were using their AA talk. I never got anywhere then. Everyone seemed to belong to a group: Alcoholics Anonymous, Jane

Fonda's Aerobics Workouts, Outward Bound. Each group had its own private jargon, which made outsiders feel as if they did not belong. They were like country clubs for poor people, with the fervor of a religious cult thrown in to the mix. I wondered how Mary would react if I told her about my amnesia, confided to her the way I might tell a mother, if I had one. Mary was something like my mother, restrained and brooding. I wondered if Mary would address me like they did each other in Friends of AA, if she would use the jargon.

The Cape highway was almost deserted at night, so the drive was easy. I caught glimpses of the lights on the marshes and inlets as I drove by, negotiated the rotaries with diligence since these circular traffic ways with their onramps and off-ramps seemed chaotic to me. Mary had fallen asleep; sometimes I looked over to make sure I had not woken her. It seemed it would take a lot of trust to give your car to someone you hardly knew and then fall asleep in it while they drove you out of town. I could never do that. But Mary was exhausted, and I was willing to drive. It was the practical solution.

The neighborhood where Mary had grown up had big trees and modest houses. I parked in the driveway behind Mary's parents' car and we went in through the kitchen door. It was a homey place with yellow tile and cantaloupes on the counter.

Upstairs all the doors and windows were open. The two twin beds in Mary's room were turned down, they had pink flowered sheets and solid pale pink spreads. While Mary was in the bathroom, I wandered around the room, inspecting the basketball and bowling trophies on the dresser and tables. I changed into a t-shirt and climbed into the bed nearest the door. Then I noticed the cigarette butts in the ashtray on the nightstand next to me, and the pillow smelled like Mary.

Mary entered the room and set her black gym back on the other bed. She was dressed in a t-shirt and her hair was damp around the edges. She climbed into the other bed, took off her watch and set it on the nightstand.

I asked her if I were in the wrong bed. She said it didn't matter. In a few minutes Mary was asleep in her sister's bed, lying on her side, facing the window. I lay on my side for a while, then the other side, then I gave up and turned over on my back where I could watch Mary sleep. I could not sleep. I was in a strange house, with Mary's parents downstairs, and Mary asleep in the bed next to me. And I was in Mary's bed.

At ten the next morning, I gave up the idea of sleeping, and went downstairs into the kitchen where Mary's parents had been talking since nine. I told them I was Kate and that I had driven Mary up.

Mary's mother said it was awfully sweet of me. She introduced herself as Ellie and her husband as Tom. We chatted about Provincetown and then Ellie and Tom went back to their bacon and eggs. Ellie had a pink curler cap on her head, and she was wearing a blue flowered smock. Her left arm was swollen. Tom had thick white hair, and a handsome face. He was short and stocky, smaller than Ellie, it seemed.

Ellie explained that she wore the cap to hide her hair, which was falling out.

After her shower, Ellie came out of the bathroom in her street clothes, without her curler cap, and showed me her thinning hair. I said it didn't look so bad. There were two crosses on the side of her head. They looked like targets.

After Mary and I had showered and changed, we went to her sister Celia's. When we got there the grown ups were congregated in the kitchen cleaning quahogs. Celia said hello and her husband hugged Mary. Ellie introduced them to me. She asked them if I wasn't sweet to drive Mary up there to see them. Celia and her husband nodded. I wondered why they had such peculiar expressions on their faces.

The two younger kids were playing video games, and I could hear them shouting in the living room. An older boy sat out on the enclosed porch watching the Red Sox game. I was opening marinated vegetables when the little girl came running in from the living room. She grabbed my hand and asked if I would play with them. Ellie warned me not to let her exhaust me. The girl dragged me out of the kitchen.

They were playing a video game where a gorilla at the top of the screen rolls basketballs down a slope. The player controls a little man at the bottom of the screen who tries to walk up the slopes, jumping over the basketballs the gorilla is rolling at him. I tried my best but I never got the little man past the first or second slope before the gorilla zapped him with one of the basketballs. The little girl and her brother could get the man all the way up the slopes to the very top. I tried a few more times, then I gave up and went out onto the porch to watch the Red Sox game.

Mary and Tom were out there with the older boy. Mary

was asking the boy which video movies he wanted her to bring up from Ethan's Pharmacy the next time she came. All three of them were drinking beers. Tom offered to get me one. Mary told him I didn't drink.

I sat down next to Tom. He offered me one of his Lucky Strikes. I said I didn't smoke.

Tom asked Mary where she found me and offered her the pack of Lucky Strikes. She took one and went in the house to find her water filters. Tom leaned over and whispered to me, "And you don't go out with boys?"

I did not know what he meant so I smiled politely and, feeling it was my responsibility to reveal a vice, confessed that I was addicted to chocolate.

Tom laughed. He said I would grow out of it. He said Mary had the same problem until she worked at the Necco factory. He asked me how old I was anyway. I said I was almost 30. He said I was ten years younger than Mary and he was seven years younger than his wife. He said it was an outrageous thing to do in those days, marry a woman seven years older than you. Now people did all sorts of outrageous things and nobody minded. He asked me if I was sure I didn't want a cigarette. I said I thought I should take a nap. Tom got up and showed me to the guest room. I lay down on the guest bed, and went to sleep.

When I woke up the little girl was shaking my arm and asking me if I wanted to play Pac-Man. She said it wasn't as hard as the gorilla and that she would teach me. I sat up. Mary was standing in the doorway. Mary told the little girl I had to go now. She said I would learn Pac-Man next time and winked at me.

When we were out on the highway, I asked Mary how

they seemed. She said that her mom was in much better spirits. Her dad wasn't pestering her mom as much to eat right, but she was worried her dad was going to be miserable once her mom was gone. He wasn't used to being alone. She thought maybe she should go to Boston for the winter. When we got back she said I could borrow the car anytime mine was broken down or needed service. That was all. Nothing happened at all. Now I was sitting at Mary's breakfast table in the middle of Harper Martin's Benefit week, staring at a protein shake.

"Harper's pre-trial negotiations are underway," she said, pointing to the television. "There's hope for a pre-trial settlement."

I nodded and looked down into the glass of brown liquid. As far as I knew, I had now done something truly unusual, and I had no idea what it was like. It gave me an odd feeling, a mixture of regret and awe.

Mary sat down at the table. "Look," she said, "I'm sorry if what I said last night was blunt, but I really can't have a one night stand. It really is what the gay boys do."

I looked up at her in wonderment. So we didn't sleep together after all.

"I'm sorry," she said, "there I go repeating the blunt thing I said. But it's true, and we had a nice talk, didn't we?"

I wondered what we talked about. I started to cry. I wondered why I couldn't remember anything if nothing had happened.

"Don't cry," she said. "Please don't cry. I'm glad you told me about your mother. It makes things easier for me." Mary held me and stroked my hair. "The whole time I was in Boston I kept thinking I wanted to see you, I wanted to talk to you, because your mother had died, and I knew you'd understand how I felt, and you wouldn't feel uncomfortable around me. You'd know how to act around me, without trying to baby me or apologize."

That was the most Mary had ever said to me.

"Have you stopped crying now?" I nodded. "So you're alright?"

"I'll be alright."

"Drink your protein shake," she said, and pushed the glass of brown liquid under my face.

"You know it looks disgusting." I sniffed at it.

"It doesn't taste bad. Try it." I took a sip. "You have to learn to forgive yourself."

"That's what you keep saying."

***

When I returned to my apartment, the door was ajar, and Gabe sat on the day bed in the kitchen, gazing up through the skylight. When he heard me come in, he leapt off the bed and shouted: "I have an idea!" Then he stopped, tilted his head to one side and looked at me inquiringly, the way a deer will, as if it understands what you've said.

"What?"

"I'm not going to ask," he said, shaking his head. "I don't even want to know."

"What's the idea?"

Gabe pulled out one of the kitchen chairs, sat me down in it, and sat down across from me on the day bed. "Phenylethylamine," he said. He pulled a newspaper article out of his pocket and unfolded it. "The chemical that's in chocolate.

It says here that 70 percent of depressed patients have lower than normal levels of phenylethylamine in the brain." I took the article and started to read it. "You're always eating chocolate. Maybe your phenylethylamine levels are too low. The phenylethylamine in chocolate makes you feel like you're in love. Maybe that's why you sleep with everyone." He pulled out another article and handed it to me. This one was about chocolate addiction.

I looked at both the articles and shook my head. "So what do you propose?" I said.

"We find a doctor to give you phenylethylamine."

"No doctors," I said, and handed him the articles.

"But Kate—"

"First off, I wouldn't pass the test for being depressed. It says here you only pass if your cortisol isn't suppressed following an ingestion of dexamethasone. Mine is. They tried that at Lahey Clinic. And even if I did pass, they don't give you the drug to cure you. They use 'successful therapies' to bring the phenyl level back up. Read what it says." I pointed to the article.

"So what's a successful therapy?" he asked, reading the article I had given back to him.

"They just talk to you and try to cheer you up. I'm telling you it won't work. Did you talk to any doctors about this?" He nodded. "Well, what did they say?"

"They said they wouldn't do it, but I bet if I found one who sympathized with your case, and thought this was a good idea—"

"You're not going to find anyone, Gabe."

He got up and went to the kitchen window. He leaned over the sink to look up at the sky, and watched the gulls fly overhead. Then he looked down into the yard, where the landlord was stacking window frames by the side of the house. "If I do, will you try it?"

"Gabriel, try to be sensible. No one is going to give me phenylethylamine. Do they even make it?"

"If it's present in chocolate, and present in your brain, they must be able to make a synthetic version."

"This is ridiculous. I feel like I'm in a Woody Allen movie or something, the one in outer space."

"*Sleepers*," he said. "Will you try it?"

"No. It's too farfetched."

"The problem is farfetched. He turned around and looked at me. Then he came back and sat down on the day bed. "You don't want to be cured, do you?" He put his hand on my knee. "Please?"

"No doctor will go along with this plan. This isn't the twenty-first century. Look, why argue about this when you haven't even found a doctor?"

He stood up and shoved the articles into his pocket. "Forget it," he said. "You don't want to be cured. I'll find something else. Maybe I'll have to trick you." He looked at me to see how I would react to this, but I had gotten up and put my head through the skylight to look out. Gabriel emitted one of his world-weary sighs, and left the apartment.

In about ten minutes he was back. "Kate, Kate," he said. He took both my hands in his and led me from the bedroom into the kitchen. "This is Eleanor," he said, indicating the Voodoo Woman, who was sitting on the day bed dressed in her scarf outfit, and adorned with bone earrings, tooth necklaces, eel-skin belts, and bronze bracelets stacked on her wrists. We shook hands; hers was bony and unusually warm.

I had never heard her called by her Christian name before. It sounded unnatural. "I've asked Eleanor if she would hypnotize you, and she's agreed."

"The doctors tried that at the Clinic. It didn't work."

"This isn't the same kind of hypnosis," he said. He looked at the Voodoo Woman.

"I was initiated by a Shaman into the healing mysteries," the Voodoo Woman said. Then she added matter-of-factly: "I can talk to the gods. I've met them." She jangled the bracelets on her wrist, as if she were calling to them to show themselves and back up her claim.

"I won't do it," I said.

Gabe walked over to the sink and looked gloomily out the window. "How can I help you if you won't try anything?"

I joined him at the window, lifted up on my toes and whispered in his ear: "But she's Looney Tunes."

Gabe whispered back: "She can't hurt you. Maybe she really can do something." He turned around and addressed the Voodoo Woman. "She'll do it," he said. "I'm going now. I'll be at the restaurant." Then he kissed me on the forehead and left before I could say anything.

"You were at Hatches Harbor," the Voodoo Woman said. She jangled her bracelets again, and then pulled on one of the teeth that were hanging around her long neck.

"You saw me?"

The Voodoo woman nodded solemnly. "I felt your presence. But don't worry, I was the only one who did."

"Were you helping them?"

"I tried to bestow the crates with a blessing of safe passage, a protection by the gods, but they stopped me." She looked up through the skylight as if she expected to see something there. "They shouldn't have stopped me. That's why the crates were taken away. An unfinished spell, even a good-intended one, is like a curse, you know."

"I didn't know," I said. It sounded like an apology.

The Voodoo Woman got up and stood next to me. She looked out through the window, then bent over slightly to lay her wrists on the porcelain sink, as if to cool her blood. "You've been with Getz," she said.

I studied her face. I did not know if this were alright to confess. "Don't worry," she said. "It is a good thing to have been with Getz. He is indelible. He leaves his mark. That is because he knows the gods."

"How does he know them?"

"He met them in the sea, one morning very early, when he was diving for lobster. He was down very deep, when he went too far, and got lost. They came to visit him then. He is very lucky to have met them."

"Raptures of the Deep. Euphoria."

The Voodoo Woman nodded.

"What about Harper?" I asked. "Does he know the gods?"

The Voodoo Woman looked out the window for a long time. Then she went back to the day bed and sat down under the skylight, so when the gulls flew over, they cast a shadow across her body. "He has their mischief," she said. "He seeks their blessing."

"And myself?" This seemed more like a tarot reading than hypnosis.

The Voodoo Woman lay down on the day bed, scattering the teeth necklace into her maze of hair. She lifted her arms up toward the skylight, sending the bronze bracelets clanking down against her elbows. "You have a magnet inside you," she said. "It's made of longing. It draws people to you."

I thought about this. "How did the magnet get there?"

"Something happened a long long time ago, that caused the gods to put it there."

"Why did they put it there?"

"I'm not sure. To protect you, maybe to punish you. Or to guide you."

She was extending her fingers toward the skylight, as if she meant to draw something in through the Plexiglas dome.

"And you?" I asked. "How did you meet the gods?"

"The Shaman made a hole through my tongue. And he gave me a string of thorns. I put the string of thorns through the hole, and tied it, so it became a circle. Then I pulled and pulled the ring of thorns through the hole in my tongue, pulled it around and around, until the gods came to me."

I shivered. It made my bones ache to think of it. I looked up at the skylight. That strange quality of light that drew painters to the Cape seemed to have descended on the window in my roof. The whole room had become a luminescent silver blue, as if it were submerged in water, where it hovered just under the surface, the sky above bright and beckoning. Then the glare increased, the room turned more and more silver, and then white, until I could only see the outline of the Voodoo Woman lying on the day bed, like a line drawing etched into a white space. A breeze began to blow softly, like the flapping of wings, as if a gull had flown through the skylight and was trapped in the apartment. The wind picked up, and the flapping increased, as if a whole flock of gulls and flown through the skylight, as if the entire space of the room had been overcome by the motion of wings, flapping around my head and arms. I found the kitchen table and sat down at it, bent forward and put my hands over my head to protect my face. But someone grasped my wrists and brought my hands away.

I looked up. It was my mother who had taken hold of my wrists and was standing over me. I could barely make her out in the silver glare and the rush of wings, but I knew it was my mother. She bent down in front of me, took my hands in hers, and kissed the palm of one and then the other, holding them against her cheek afterward, and leaning against them as if she sought some kind of rest there. Then she placed her head in my lap and began to cry.

"What do you want?" I said. I rested my hand on my mother's back, as if to test her breathing. "What do you want?" But my mother didn't answer. She just cried.

The next thing I knew the room had become its normal color again, the skylight was closed, and the Voodoo Woman sat across from me on the day bed, with her head cocked like a bird. "Who was it?" she said.

"My mother. I asked her what she wanted."

"Did she tell you?" I shook my head. "Was she a very quiet person in life? Didn't give much away?"

"She was very restrained. She would never say what she was feeling."

"People don't change after they die." She sighed. "I'm sorry. I wish I could help you more." The Voodoo Woman rested her hand on my shoulder.

I looked up at the skylight, as if I half-believed my mother would come back, and I would get another chance to talk to her. I had not expected her the first time. "Will she come back?" I asked. "Can you bring her back?"

"No. She won't come again."

"I wasn't ready. You should have told me she was coming."

The Voodoo Woman got up to leave. "I didn't know," she said. "I only bring the light. I don't know what will come inside of it. That is up to you."

After the Voodoo Woman had left, I went into the bedroom and retrieved the skin-suit man from his hiding place. I sat for a long time and watched him, resting in the palms of my hands. I tried to imagine how it felt to be inside someone else's skin. I tried to imagine my skin wrapped around another. I thought, *And this is how he gained his magic. This is how he let the god inside him.*

***

It was just past noon when I walked out on the wharf to board the whale watch boat. The water glittered all around me; the sun seemed especially bright against it and hurt my eyes if I tried to look at the reflections. Someone stood on the dock waving at me. If I squinted into the glare, I could barely discern his dark form, dusted grey in the middle, like a charcoal drawing of a man whose face has been rubbed out. But I knew it was Gabe; he was waiting for me.

"What happened?" he said when I was within earshot.

"I tried it." When I was standing next to him I laid my head on his shoulder for a moment, then lifted it, and looked him right in the face.

"Can you remember everything now?" he said. He held

his hand to my neck, as if to take my pulse. I shook my head. "Well did anything happen? Did you resist?"

"My mother appeared."

"What did she say?"

"Nothing." I was not going to tell him that my mother was very sad about something; that she had cried in my arms.

"Well, how do you feel?" he asked. He ran his hand up and down my arm. "You look pallid."

I shrugged. "I don't know. Is the light funny today? I feel dizzy."

Gabe looked up at the sky. "Not especially. Are you sure you should go out on the boat?"

I looked over at the whale watch boat, The Dolphin II, which was docked next to us. Tourists were positioning themselves along the wooden railings and adjusting the lenses of their cameras. Getz stood near the gangplank. He leaned against the rail, smoking a Camel unfiltered and watched me scrupulously, as if he were a private detective, hired by my husband to find out why I was so listless, went for long walks in the evenings and no longer paid any attention to him. "Why not?" I said. It sounded more like a dare than a question.

Gabe kissed me goodbye and waited till I had boarded the boat before he turned to leave. He took a few steps and came back again. They were pulling up the gangplank. "Are you sure?" he yelled. When I did not answer he turned and walked away.

Getz dropped the butt of his cigarette in the water and lit another one. "What's with him?" he said, motioning the new cigarette at Gabe.

"He's just worried." I looked at Getz, tracing the sharp

lines in his face. He was so handsome, and so severe—he unsettled me. I wished I could remember.

"What's with you?" he asked. "You look like you've seen God."

"Not quite."

He looked at me oddly, as if he wanted to know what I meant, but thought it would be a breach of privacy to ask.

"Well, Angelo's a nervous wreck," he said. "We better go find him and just hang around where he can see us."

He took my arm and led me around toward the front of the boat. It was much larger than I had expected. A jazz band played on the upper deck, and a bar was set up nearby, where the tourists bought Cape Codders and then lingered near the clarinet player, watching him wince and contort his shoulders to elicit the raunchy high notes, casting furtive glances at the water and the receding shoreline. I stood next to the rail and looked back at the town. It seemed precious from far away, so diminutive and harmless, like an architect's model or a toy.

"Thank God you came," Angelo said, coming up behind me at the rail, and clapping me on the back. I looked at him with puzzlement; I did not know why I had suddenly become so necessary. Angelo followed the camera crew around, showing them where to lay cables so the tourists would not trip over them. While he directed them, he fiddled with his cameras, loading and unloading them, pulling canisters of film out of his pockets, changing lenses, looking through the different colored filters. When he noticed me leaning quietly against the rail, watching him, he said, "Stay right there; don't go away," as if he expected me to bolt the minute I was out of his sight. Getz came up and stood next to me like a guard, smoking one cigarette after another, looking at me intensely and not saying anything, as if conversation would be false or useless to him today, when he was surrounded by water, heading out to sea. But then, Getz never said much anyway. He stared into his drink or at the smoke curling up from the tip of his burning cigarette and appeared to brood.

When the cameramen were set up, they picked a spot at the front of the boat, installed Angelo amidst the quaint disarray of ropes, nets, tackle and rigging, with his cameras strapped across his chest, and introduced him to the viewers. They asked him about his background in marine biology, his studies of seals and his interests in whales. Then they pulled the camera back and trailed him while he ran around the boat holding the megaphone to his mouth, charming the tourists with the history of the Cape end, stories of shipwrecks and whaling catastrophes, until they would reach the area out past Race Point where they were most likely to see the whales.

I wandered to the back of the boat, and watched Provincetown become smaller and smaller, until it was simply a point on the horizon, indistinguishable from all the others, unless you knew it was there. I wondered at this, at how easy it was to obliterate something just by moving away from it. Is this how I had dissolved my memory, by casting out, traveling farther and farther, until the thing I wanted to forget was just a blur, a moment indistinguishable from all the others, rubbed out, like Gabe's form beneath the glare of the sunlight? And if so, how did I find my way back, back to that moment I had succeeded so diligently in forgetting, the moment when my mother told me something I did not want to hear?

I felt I was being watched, and turned around. Getz was standing at a polite distance a few yards off, leaning against the wall of the cabin, his eyes fixed on me. He approached me now and stood next to me at the rail, staring down into the water, the way he stared at his drink or his cigarette. "Have you ever just watched the water?" he said. "I can do it for hours. I get lost in it." He gazed down at the dips, pools, whorls and currents as if he were in love. The light reflected up into his face and shimmered there, like an answer. "Have you ever tried it?" I shook my head. "You should. You lose yourself. It's soothing, like the difference between being conscious and self conscious."

The sun was still too bright for me. Everything around me—the railing, the planks beneath my feet, the sky, Getz's arm next to mine—appeared raw and overexposed. I looked down into the water and tried to forget myself. The glare was almost blinding, and soon, that was all I could see, a bright luminescent silver that slid and shifted rhythmically with the motions of the water, lulling me, tempting me into abandonment, so that when the upheaval came, just the slightest lifting up, the gentlest pressure on my arms and legs, and then the soft quick falling, it was almost imperceptible, and I lay floating naturally in the water, just as calm and as absent as I had been looking down into it, the happy silver glare all around me, the gentle lapping about my ears like contented murmurs, a purr of oblivion. If I had thought about anything then, lying in the current with no notion of danger or death, I would have known that this was oblivion, and oblivion was the peace and satisfaction, the rest from longing and desire, the surfeit I had been seeking all along, and had never found until that moment.

The shouting brought me back to consciousness. I looked up and saw the back of the boat at a distance, the tiny people at the railing in their brightly colored shirts, waving and shouting: "Killer Whale! Killer Whale!" throwing ropes and life preservers into the water. They looked precious, the way Provincetown looked when the boat had drawn away from shore.

I looked up at the sun. I did not want this, the noise and commotion, the running and shouting. I wanted to go away again, into that peaceful place the glare had sent me, where I was finally satisfied. I stared at the sun for a while, and felt as if I were losing myself again, going under, back into oblivion. I even felt that gentle lifting, as if something good intentioned was displacing me. This almost convinced me I would return to that place, but the shrieks from the boat grew even louder. I opened my eyes just as I felt my head break the surface of the water. I blew the water out of my mouth by instinct, and looked around. They were throwing a small life raft into the water. I could see Angelo at the rail holding the megaphone.

"Kate!" he shouted. "Don't be afraid. The whale won't hurt you. It's trying to keep you afloat."

I peered down into the water. My arms and legs were now too numb from the cold to actually feel, and it gave me an odd sensation to see them treading water, when I could not sense the swoosh of the currents. On my left, out of my side vision, I caught a swatch of white pass by, and then a dark body of black follow on top of it. Even this close in the water, the animal seemed too small to be a whale, too nimble and sprightly, as if it had some playful mischief in mind. I watched it circle, surface, breach, and dive again, and tried to follow its course underneath and around me. It was much too small and sleek to be a whale, I decided, and it had that bright white patch underneath its head. It looked more like a dolphin.

"Kate!" Angelo shouted again. "It's the orca that was hanging around the harbor a few weeks ago. It will let you swim with it. Grab hold of the fin. Put your hand on the fin."

It seemed like the simplest thing in the world to do —grab on to the fin. I only had to reach out my hand and catch hold of it, and the animal would do the rest. I looked around at the water, at the bright sun, at my own disembodied limbs below, treading to keep me afloat, and I wondered at how arbitrary it all was. I was not sure I wanted to go back, but if I grabbed hold of its fin, the dolphin would take me, and if I did not, the dolphin would just go for a swim, expend its mischief.

While I tried to make up my mind, the dolphin circled, and the tourists yelled from the boat, and Getz climbed down a ladder into the raft to come after me. In the end it was not really a decision; they weren't going to allow me my oblivion. All I did was reach out my hand, and the dolphin took me.

***

When I woke up in the projection booth of the Bad Attitude Cinema I was sitting in a director's chair, wrapped in blankets. Joe, Getz and Gabe stood around me like the Trinity, talking about the Orca, but when they saw I had moved and opened my eyes they all stopped and stared at me, waiting for me to speak. It reminded me of the end of *The Wizard of*

Oz, when Dorothy wakes up from her knock on the head and everyone who had been in her dream is standing around her bed. I wanted to recite Dorothy's speech, tell them I had visited a magical land and they were all in it. But instead I said, "See any whales? What time is it? What am I doing here?"

"These are all rhetorical questions," Lance shouted from the balcony. "Sounds like she's awake."

"Don't pay any attention to him," Gabe said. "He's full of himself. He's been hired on as a consultant to make a Hollywood feature film about Harper Martin."

"How'd he get that?" I said.

"Through one of Angelo's CBS cameramen. They're out there right now, talking about the deal."

"Lance has Hollywood written all over him," Joe said.

"Why do they want Lance?" I said.

"He was born here," Gabe said. "His mother was born here. His grandmother was born here. They want a Provincetown expert."

"You can trace his family all the way back to the Pilgrims," Getz said.

"He wanted to get into film making anyway, so they figured they'd hire him cheap, and he'll get the experience he needs," Joe explained.

"Thank God," Gabe said. "He never would have gone to film school. But now look at him; he's full of himself."

They glanced out the door of the projection room and watched Lance talk to Angelo. Lance was dancing with a director's chair, imitating Fred Astaire's dance with the hat rack in *Royal Wedding*. Then he jumped up into it, sat down on his knees, and began to sing "I'm Putting All My Eggs In One Basket."

"So how'd the filming of the whale watch go?" I said, looking up at them and adjusting my blankets to keep warm.

"You were the star catastrophe," Getz said patting me on the shoulder. "After that it kind of went downhill."

"Did you see any whales?" I asked. "Or did you have to take me back to shore?"

"The Rescue Squad picked you up in a helicopter," Getz said. "We saw a few whales after that; the clarinet player always draws a crowd."

"People really pay all that money for a whale watch tour just to hear the clarinet player?" Gabe said.

"No," Getz said. "The clarinet player draws a crowd of whales."

"Why would they like the clarinet player?" I said.

"I don't know," Getz said. "They like that sultry stuff he cranks out."

"I wonder why whales like the clarinet," Gabe said.

"Just *his* clarinet," Getz said. "The same thing happens if that guy plays the sax. It has to be that guy."

"He was good," I said. The three men looked at me as if I'd just come back from Mars. "So what am I doing here anyway?" I added, pulling at the blankets. "I mean, how come I'm not at home?"

"You were at home," Gabe said. "But you kept saying you didn't want to miss the Benefit screening of the *Rocky Horror Picture Show*, and you were afraid everyone was going to leave you alone, so we brought you here."

"The Rescue Squad guys say it's safer anyway," Getz said, "since they're right downstairs in Pumper Number Two."

"Yeah, screwing up my sound system with their dispatch radio," Joe said.

"Safer?" I said. "Why safer?"

"You might go into shock," Gabe said.

There was an awkward silence while we all looked at each other.

"Well, I better get moving," Joe said. "The film canisters are downstairs." He stroked his glove and walked to the door. Getz followed him, offering to give him a hand. "Don't overdo it," Joe said to me, and the two men left together.

When they had gone and I was alone with Gabe, I said, "Why do I get the feeling that this whole thing was planned?" I repositioned myself in the director's chair to try and get comfortable, but nothing worked; all my limbs ached from treading water.

"I talked to your doctor at the Lahey Clinic," he said. He leaned against the counter where the spare reels were stacked and crossed his arms against his chest. "He told me they'd tried just about everything, but a trauma might restore your memory. I decided to try the hypnosis first, and if that didn't work—well, I knew you could swim, the way you're always talking about that pool you had in the backyard in Los Angeles when you were a kid, and how your mom hated pools and would come out to the yard every evening at dinner time and stand at the coping just smoking a cigarette and not say anything until you got out of the pool, and then she would wrap the towel around you and take you back into the house."

He stopped talking. I couldn't remember telling him about my mother and the pool.

"You were never in any danger," he said. "Getz knew about it, and so did Angelo. They weren't going to let you get into any trouble out there. Getz is a scuba diver, you know."

"Did you tell them about my amnesia? Did you tell the Voodoo Woman?" He said no. "So how were you so sure I'd fall overboard? Did you drug me or something?"

He laughed. "You've been watching too many movies. Getz dropped you over."

"Getz dropped me!"

"It was the safest way. He could pick the moment; he would be ready."

"There could have been sharks in the water."

"There weren't any sharks. He saw the Orca. He dropped you in on purpose then. It was safer that way."

"A killer whale!"

"They just call them that. It's just a dolphin. They don't eat people. You knew that. It's been in the bay the last few weeks. It's practically a domesticated animal. The Provincetown mascot."

"I didn't agree to this, you know," I said.

"How can you volunteer for a life threatening experience? It had to be a surprise. You had to think you were in danger. Of course, you weren't. We knew that."

"Great."

"So can you remember everything now? Did your whole life come flashing before you in that moment when you thought you were drowning?"

"It was very peaceful. I didn't remember anything. My mind was a total blank."

He stood up and paced around the projection room, tapping on the posters as he went by them. "You're hopeless," he said. "You're absolutely hopeless."

"I know."

He walked to the door. "I'm going now. Lance and Angelo

are right out here if you need them. And the Rescue Squad is just downstairs. Joe and Getz should be back with the movie reels in a minute." He peered down the stairs.

"What time is it? Aren't you going to stay and see *Rocky Horror*?"

"Eleven-thirty. I'm going home to bed. You want to meet me there afterward? I can keep my eye on you that way. The doctor said not to leave you alone until morning." I said I would meet him after the show. "Get Lance or Getz to drive you over. You shouldn't walk that far." He smiled sadly at me, and left. I could hear him talking to Joe and Getz on the stairs as he went down.

They hauled the film canisters inside the projection room; Joe took the reels out and shelved them in the racks so they'd be ready to use, and began to set the first two up on the projectors, threading the film between the lenses and bobbins, testing the sound system and lights. He checked on me now and then, looking over at me as if he thought I might disappear. Finally, he said, "What was the ride like?" and gave me an embarrassed smile.

"The ride?" I said.

"Getz says you hitched a ride with that dolphin that's been hanging out by the wharf lately. I heard it was really something."

I thought about the ride with the dolphin. I didn't know how to explain it.

Getz carried in the last few canisters of film, set them down on the counter for Joe, took one look at me and said, "Now you look like you really have seen God."

"Not quite."

Angelo and Lance came bustling in to the projection

room. Lance waltzed around my director's chair singing "Dancing Cheek to Cheek," then bowed gravely in front of me and kissed my hand. "Kate, Kate, feeling better?" Angelo said. "Can we talk?"

"Talk to me, talk to me," Lance drawled in a fake Brooklyn-ese.

"Could you guys take her out on the balcony?" Joe said. "I don't have enough room in here, and it's going to get hot when I crank up these monsters." He pointed to the film projectors.

Getz and Angelo picked up the arms of my director's chair, carried me out onto the balcony and set me down facing the screen. Lance waved his arms like a flagman directing a jet down onto an aircraft carrier, then lapsed into some fake karate punches and kicks, and fell down, supposedly insensible, on the balcony floor.

"I've never seen him so happy," I said.

"He has a job," Angelo said. He readjusted my blankets. "Warm enough?"

I nodded. "So how did the filming go? Getz here told me you saw some whales after the Rescue Squad carted me away. And why do the whales like that clarinet player so much?"

Angelo shrugged. "One of the Mysteries of Life."

Getz had been twirling his cigarette between his fingers and fidgeting as if he wanted to object. "Come on, Kate," he said. "You told me yourself that after your mom died your cat used to sit in the front windowsill and wait for her to come home, and when she didn't it would whimper."

I nodded my head. Of course, I didn't remember.

Getz and Angelo leaned against the half-wall of the balcony and watched the people come into the movie theatre, carrying the props they needed for their role in *The Rocky Horror Picture Show*: squirt bottles filled with water, toilet paper, flashlights and cigarette lighters, powdered baby laxatives, and copies of the *Herald Tribune*. Some were dressed as the transvestite in a black corset, garters, tights, and stiletto heels; others came as the servant, copying his hunchback and domed bald head, with the yellow hair sprouting out at ear level down to his shoulders. They arrived in large parties of six or even ten more, and sat in clusters by the aisle, so it would be within close reach when the moment came to dance the Time Warp or run up onto the stage to run their fingers along the screen when Susan Sarandon sang "Toucha Toucha Toucha Touch Me."

"Here they come," Lance said.

"Whoopeee," Joe called from inside the projection room.

"I'm sorry," I said to Angelo. "I got started on the clarinet player and never gave you a chance to tell me how the filming went."

"It went well. CBS took some great footage of you with the dolphin. They want to use it in the documentary." He adjusted my blankets again. "With your permission."

"Don't do it, Kate," Lance said. He swaggered up to us, carrying a small wooden box in his hand. "I'll make a whole movie of you with the goddamned dolphin. A major feature film. We'll go to Hollywood together, you and me, no shenanigans. We'll make those fans do some serious groveling at your feet. What was that film they made with Sophia Loren in Greece? *The Boy and the Dolphin?* That's where we'll film it. In Greece. To hell with these cold climates." He opened the box and offered everyone a cigar. "From Savannah. Can't beat 'em." He put an unlit cigar in his mouth, chewed on the end, and practiced swaggering around like a gangster.

"He's too much," I said.

"Will you think about it?" Angelo said. I nodded. "I bet no one's told you the Mother of the Year's news either. She's been hired by the Casablancas modeling agency in Paris. Someone must have seen her on the news in those clips of the Bocce Tournament, or the Fashion show."

Joe had run downstairs, leapt on stage and delivered his warning speech: No baby laxatives, no open flames, no touching the screen. Then he had run back and started the movie rolling. A large pair of disembodied red lips had appeared on the black screen, and they were singing the homage to sci fi and horror flicks, of which this movie was both a tribute and a parody.

"Where is everybody?" I said.

"What do you mean?" Getz said. "The theatre is full."

"Where's Lydia Street, Antaeus, and all those people?"

"Antaeus is getting his new gallery ready for Cosmo's show," Angelo said. "The rest of them are just tired. They'll be at Cosmo's opening tomorrow."

We watched the movie for a while. Brad and Janet, two all-American kids, had a flat tire driving to see Brad's professor Dr. Scott (the audience launches their rolls of toilet paper and yells: *Great Scott!* when he's mentioned). So they get out of the car in the pouring rain, put copies of the *Herald Tribune* over their heads and walk to the ghoulish mansion that all the bikers have been driving past them to get to, where the servant is waiting in an upstairs window, singing "There's a Light Over at the Frankenstein Place." Brad and Janet join in. Tonight the audience assisted as usual, covering their heads with newspapers, squirting water into the air to fall down on the papers, and illuminating flashlights or candles, while they sang along. Getz leaned over the balcony to watch them. "And to think this has been going on for ten years," he said.

"Do you know about this movie?" Lance said. "It wasn't making any money at all when it first came out. That guy there, the blond who plays the servant, he wrote it. He sings the first song, the one with the lips, that's his voice. Anyway, it wasn't making any money, so they gave the movie to a different marketing guy, and he decided to put it on at midnight. Bam, instant success. A cult movie for teenagers. Then the whole participatory ritual developed. And the guy, Tim Curry, who plays the transvestite, he's with the Royal Shakespeare Company."

The revelers at the party had already danced the Time Warp, and the dedicated participants in the audience had danced it in the aisles with them. Now the transvestite in question was descending from his laboratory in the elevator. Janet screamed when she saw him prance out of the elevator. He threw off his cape and belted out his "I'm Just A Sweet Transvestite from Transsexual Transylvania" number, slithered back into the elevator, from where he delivered his famous speech, inviting Brad and Janet to: *come up to the lab, and see what's on the slab.*

"Listen to that modulation, pacing, tonal quality," Lance said. "What control. Only a guy from the Royal Shakespeare Company could deliver those lines like that."

"That's my favorite part," I said.

"Well scrape my uterus," he said, and offered me a cigar. But I didn't take one because I was about to fall asleep. I slept through the whole movie; Lance wanted to wake me up for the very end, where the transvestite and the muscle man he had created in the laboratory fall off the RKO tower into the pool, and swim around like water sprites with Brad and Janet, while they sing: "Don't Dream It, Be It"; but Joe wouldn't allow it, so they let me sleep.

***

Saturday

When I woke up Saturday morning I was at home, in bed with Joe Houston. Joe looked peaceful curled up on his side, his black-gloved hand resting on the pillow close to his face. I started to get up when I noticed Gabriel standing in the doorway between the bedroom and kitchen.

"I'm sorry," I said. "I really don't know how this happened."

"It doesn't matter," Gabe said. "Just get dressed. I want to show you something." He sounded resigned, and this made me feel even worse.

The voices had wakened Joe and he turned over on his back. When he saw Gabe, he said, "No scenes this time"—and held up his hands as if he were at gunpoint.

Gabe shook his head. "No scenes," he repeated, and disappeared into the kitchen. Joe and I heard the skylight crank open, then the tap water began to run in the sink and the dishes crashed and clattered. "Sorry, babe," Joe said, and kissed me lightly on the tip of the nose. He turned over and went back to sleep. When I got out of the shower I found him in the same position, curled up and snoring. Gabe was waiting in the newly cleaned kitchen, standing next to the dish drainer, watching the plates drip dry. He asked me if I was ready to leave.

To get where we were going we had to ride in Gabe's truck. He drove us out beyond the Beech Forest through the dunes of the Provincelands to the edge of the National Seashore, and across some newly laid roads. He did not say much, and I did not feel inclined to talk. I enjoyed driving, the limbo of being nowhere, just moving forward, leaving things behind. Gabe parked the truck in front of a vacant lot, in one of the new tracts adjacent to the Provincelands. I followed him past the scrub pines and flagged markers up a grade to a leveled area about the size of a one-car garage. Then he disappeared behind a pile of sand, and reappeared above me, on the hill to the west, which was also level on top. "You can even see the water," he said. I followed him.

The view was spectacular. From up there you could see everything: the beige and cream colored dunes, the rust and burgundy brush of the Provincelands, the grey-green water of the bay beyond. To the north the ranger station at Race Point was in view on the horizon line, and to the south, following the highway down cape, the water towers on the edge of town could be seen. Only the town itself was hidden by a new house, which was being built across the street. Standing there in the wind, looking out across the dunes to the sea, I could almost believe this was the end of the world, somewhere peaceful, where I could be happy.

"A guy offered me a quarter of a million dollars for this property yesterday," he said.

"This is your land?" I said, incredulous, spreading out my arms to fan the air. "This?"

He nodded. "Last month it was only worth 50,000."

"Are you going to sell it?"

He knelt down and examined a sapling that was growing at the edge of the property line. "I'm going to start selling my designs again, and use the money to build a house. I should have done it a long time ago."

He stood up, walked to the front edge of the hill, and inspected the house that was being built across the street. Then he walked toward the back, examining the old trees and brush along the leveled hill. When he reached me he stopped and scanned the horizon. Then he took my hand. I decided right then that if he asked me to marry him I would say yes, and never cheat on him again.

"I brought you here to tell you that I can't see you anymore," he said. He sat down in the sand and pulled on my hand until I sat down beside him.

"I'll try the phenylethylamine if you want," I said. He had been so nice to me; he had tried so hard, and now, suddenly, he looked so lost, as if someone had died and left him alone. So it was the same predicament after all, the one I had faced with Cedric. Gabe could not continue with me knowing I did not remember our intimacies. So I had been right in sleeping with Joe and Getz and Harper, in distancing Gabe. He would have left me anyway.

"It's not the amnesia," he said. He put his arm around me. "I don't mind that." He looked me in the eye. He could tell I did not believe him.

"Then what is it?"

"I'm jealous," he said matter-of-factly. "You keep sleeping with other people."

"I intended not to sleep with other people after you asked me. But it just kept happening. I just kept waking up with other people. Since I can't remember, I don't know how it happens."

"It doesn't matter now. My feelings are too hurt. Don't you understand? Hasn't anyone ever made you jealous?"

"Of course. A million times."

"Not here. Not in Provincetown."

"What about Cedric? He left me for someone else."

"Did you cheat on him?" I shook my head. "Then why did you cheat on me so much?" I said I didn't know. "Is it because Cedric left you?"

"I don't know. Maybe."

We sat for a while, huddled next to each other against the wind, and did not say anything. Finally I asked: "So that's it? There's nothing I can do? I can't try again?"

He shook his head. "My feelings are too hurt. I can't take it anymore."

I leaned my head on his shoulder. He asked me what I was thinking. I said, "This never would have happened if only I could remember."

"It's not the amnesia, Kate. That doesn't matter. But I can't live with being jealous and having my feelings hurt all the time." He looked at me and saw that I still did not believe him.

"I'm sorry," I said weakly.

"I know. I don't hold a grudge."

I looked at him. I knew he didn't. "Can I ask you something?" He nodded. "What happened that night with you and Joe that everyone's always referring to?"

Gabe laughed and brushed the hair out of his eyes. "I walked you home. When we got there Joe was asleep in your bed with just his glove on. I woke him up and we yelled at each other for a while, then I left. That's all." He looked down and poked his finger into the sand under his foot.

"I'm sorry," I said again. I shook my head. "I'm really sorry."

He took his finger out of the sand and looked over at me. "I've already forgiven you," he said. I leaned my head on his shoulder and he kissed it.

***

Sunday

By the time Cosmo's show opened, every wall in Antaeus' new gallery was hung with Cosmo's paintings. Even after the guests had arrived for the opening, and were milling around with glasses of champagne in their hands perusing the new canvases, Antaeus and Cosmo were still shuttling the modular walls into different positions, like young boys continually changing the layout of the tracks on their new train set. Antaeus' carpenter followed them around diligently with a ladder, readjusting the ceiling lights so the paintings would be properly illuminated. Eventually the gallery was so full of people it became dangerous to try to move the walls and ladder through the crowds, so Antaeus relinquished his plans, and they left the modular walls where they were. The carpenter retired his ladder behind the door next to the bar, and poured himself a bourbon.

Of Cosmo's new paintings the nudes drew the most commentary, because they were unexpected. Blaine said Cosmo hadn't painted nudes since Nello's wife left him, and their restaurant partnership dissolved. There was a considerable amount of speculation on who modeled for the new canvases, since, as Lance pointed out, the same woman appeared in all of them, like a recurring theme. Raphael and some others said they recognized The Voodoo Woman in the pictures, but Lydia and Edward the real estate agent thought a stranger from out of town had posed. The seascapes of Long Point and Hatches Harbor were predictable, the same flat blue and grey washes that he had been painting since his art student days in Rhode Island, but the locals expected these pictures, and Angelo was not alone when he said he was fond of them despite his esthetic judgment. Discussion was brisk and pointed around the still lives. He had developed a new style reminiscent of Picasso and Braque, with disembodied heads sitting on tables, pedestals and guitars thrown in haphazardly, slabs of color, dividing lines, chairs and window frames giving the composition a geometric flavor. Some of the critics, including Joe and Getz, said these canvases showed too much homage to the early Cubists.

Those who weren't examining the paintings, taking air on the porch, or arguing around the hors d'oeuvres, had congregated at the bar, where the television was on, and tuned to the *CBS Evening News* with Dan Rather. On the Temple of the Jaguars update the day before, Dan had told the viewers that the pre-trial arbitration for Harper Martin continued, and that reliable sources had told CBS News that the judge and two teams of lawyers had literally remained in the conference room day and night, only stopping for brief rests, and sending out for coffee, sandwiches, and extra files and papers. This had raised some people's hopes, among them Elaine Barry, that the federal government wanted to settle the case as quickly as possible, to quell the growing sentiment against United States military involvement in Nicaragua, a sentiment they believed was strengthened by the press coverage of the Harper Martin case.

I had been standing at the bar watching the CBS News, but when I noticed Grace was heading toward me, I slipped away, through an adjacent door. The area inside seemed like an entryway with supplies stacked along the walls. Another door opened in to a small room where a desk and file cabinet had been arranged—the office for the new gallery. Across from it, a brand new stairway led up to the new roof.

Except for the Pilgrim's Monument, no building was higher than the roof of Antaeus' new gallery, so when I ascended the stairs and emerged on the landing that had been built at the top, I could see all the other rooftops below me. I had expected to find the roof tarred, with perhaps a layer of wood planks over that to make a sundeck, but instead the entire roof had been subdivided with wooden beams, like the foundation to a house, and in among the divisions, pipes, tubes and wires had been installed. I didn't know what to make of it.

"It isn't code," someone said from down below me. I looked into the stairwell and saw Grace coming up, carrying two glasses of champagne. When she reached the top, she handed one glass to me, and then clinked it against her own. "Cheers," she said.

"Fire code?" I said, looking around.

"Building code," she said, surveying the plumbing and wiring. "He barely got permission to build the gallery on top of the cinema. I mean, just look, he's already higher than anyone else in town. Nobody knows he's building a penthouse apartment on top of that. Jesus Christ, it's like the Empire State Building. I call it the Antpire State Building.

In private, of course." She clinked her glass against mine again, as if to seal the pact of secrecy.

"A penthouse apartment!" I said. "Is that what this is?"

Grace put her index finger to her lips to assure silence, and then, balancing carefully on the crossbeams, walked through the apartment, pointing out the kitchen on the north side, the living room to the south, the bedrooms on the west, each with its own bathroom, the private screening room for films, the mini gallery, and exercise room to the east, and porches all the way around. "Imagine the view from this bathtub," she said, stepping gingerly onto a spot and waving her champagne glass at the view. "But you can't tell a soul, not a soul. They won't know a thing until the wall frames go up, and by then it will be too late."

"Why are you protecting him?" I asked. I was more curious to know why Grace was confiding in me, but I was afraid to ask that.

"We all protect each other," she said, wading back carefully across the beams toward me. "Or we try, anyway. That is what my little outburst was all about."

"Oh." I took a sip of my champagne before remembering that I usually didn't drink.

"Welcome to the club," she said, put her arm around me, and gave me a little squeeze.

"Thanks." I wanted to say I was sorry Mary wasn't interested in Grace, instead of those young girls who left Mary in the summer, but I was afraid Grace would think I was being sarcastic, so I didn't say anything.

"We better go back before someone spots us," she said, and started down, turning now and then, to make sure I was following her.

When we returned downstairs, she took up a position at the bar to watch the news, and I decided to roam the gallery again, to hear what would be said about the canvases now that the guests were well fed, had too much to drink, and had sunk into a state of complacency that was prone to revelation. I was standing in front of a still life painting in which a bust resembling the Voodoo Woman sat on a table with a vase and bowl of fruit and stared out the window at a whole woman, who resembled the bust, and was reaching up to pluck an orange off a tree, when Lance approached me and said, "There's been some revisionist theory on this one." He tapped the picture frame proprietarily.

"I suspected as much. Go ahead. Dish it."

"The Garden of Eden theme, before and after The Fall."

"I see." I nodded and stroked my chin. Antaeus came up to us bearing a champagne bottle and refilled my glass. I thanked him.

"You were supposed to let me pour your first one," he said, "but I'll let it go by this time." He clinked the bottle against my glass. "Thanks again for your help with the liquor license appeal." He watched me drink, then refilled Lance's glass. "An unappreciated genius, don't you think?" he added, tilting his forehead toward the canvas.

"He's appreciated," Lance said, "just not in the right circles." Antaeus let loose one of his uncontrollable laughs, a laugh that sounded like relief, and walked off to fill other champagne glasses. When he was out of earshot Lance said, "What do you think of the penthouse?" I furrowed my brow and tried to look puzzled but Lance just smirked. "Alright," he said, "I'll tell you something you *really* don't know."

"Do I want to know?" I said.

"Of course not. If you did, what fun would there be in telling you?" He took a sip of his champagne. "See the Mother of the Year, and the Yeast Infection, over there?"

I nodded. Lance sometimes referred to the Voodoo Woman as the Yeast Infection. "Well, they're finally leaving Antaeus. The Mother of the Year is going to Paris to model with the Casablancas Agency, and The Voodoo Woman is going with her."

"I know," I said.

"But do you know what that means? It means that, once Antaeus gets his penthouse apartment built, he's going to have to find new imbroglios to people it with."

I nodded. We looked around absently, as if we were suddenly bewildered. I tried to imagine Antaeus' penthouse peopled with imbroglios. It was easy—the whole town was like that. My life was the same way.

Lance noticed Cosmo approaching them. "Uh oh," he said, "it's the man himself," and slipped away behind *The Garden of Eden: Before and After*, which was mounted on one of the free-standing walls.

Cosmo clinked his glass against mine. "Cheers," he said.

"I like the new work," I said, motioning toward *The Garden of Eden*.

He nodded and looked around distractedly. "Nichole hasn't shown up yet," he said flatly, so it was neither a question nor a statement.

"She's coming?" I said, and then realized my mistake.

"You haven't talked to her then?" Blaine came by just then, refilling glasses, and Cosmo held his out to her.

"No, I've been meaning to stop by the house."

Cosmo looked at his shoes. "So have I."

Blaine held the champagne bottle too high, as if she were displaying it. "If you mean Nichole, she's at the bar."

The three of us watched Nichole procure a drink from the bartender. She joked with Grace and Elaine, pointed to the television set and said something that made them all laugh.

Blaine attracted Nichole's attention by waving the champagne bottle at her. Nichole made excuses at the bar and started over to them, greeting people, stopping to tease others, and exchanging pleasantries along the way, as she had when she hostessed at the restaurant, making everyone feel welcome, feel that they belonged, that they were smarter and handsomer and more accomplished than they had realized. Nichole had always been good at that.

"I guess everything goes on without me," Nichole said when she reached us.

"Not exactly," I said.

"What do you mean?" she asked. "You're still introducing innocents to dykes at the bar, still sleeping with everything that wears a front zipper—"

"Nichole," Blaine said, and laid her hand across Nichole's wrist like a reproach.

"And my father here is still as hypocritical as ever," Nichole waved her glass around. "Expounding the Protestant virtues of home, family and fidelity, then cheating on his wife and when he gets caught, chastising his mistress and exiling her from town, as if she were the only one who had bothered to participate in the crime."

"Don't," Blaine said. "Please." She knocked the champagne glass against her own thigh, as a sort of frustrated plea.

Nichole looked around the gallery. Then she looked at the painting, *The Garden of Eden: Before and After.* "I despise you," she told her father evenly. "You reek of dishonesty and hubris." Then she began to shout, and everyone in the gallery stopped what they were doing to look at her. "I despise all you people and your petty squabbles, your backbiting and your vicious senseless gossip. Who are you to judge me? Who the fuck do you think you are? God, how I hate this town of Puritans, masquerading as Bohemians."

Nichole tossed her drink down. She didn't throw it at me, she didn't really fling it into Cosmo's face, though part of it splattered and landed on his goatee. She just let the glass fly. Then she turned and walked from the gallery with such a fierce grievance in her expression that no one dared stop her.

The minute Nichole had left, the bar erupted into total chaos. People were shouting, pouring champagne on each other's heads, jumping up and down. The revelry spread to the hors d'oeuvres table, where a chorus of "God Save the Queen" struck up, followed by the "Marseillaise" and a cacophony of high school anthems. Cosmo and I couldn't imagine what they would be celebrating, until Lance brought us the news: the Harper Martin case had been settled in pre-trial arbitration.

"This bites the hairy wet one," Lance said, and then explained that Harper had been found guilty of U.S. Trade violations and U.S. Customs violations, he would be fined, and also pay fees and surcharges, the amounts of which were undisclosed, but there would be no jail term. The government had returned the crates of figurines to Harper's art dealer and Harper had been released in Manhattan. His current whereabouts were unknown, and he had not yet talked to reporters, but the government spokesman said that Harper planned to return to Provincetown briefly to arrange for painting assistants before going to Malibu, California, to begin work on the mural in the Temple of the Jaguars at the Getty Museum.

"They haven't shown Harper on the TV," he said, "but they're promising a special report on recreating the Temple of the Jaguar murals."

"No jail term," I said.

"No jury trial," Cosmo said. "I wonder what they're going to do with all the Defense Fund money from this Benefit Week we've been having. Ruth and that New York lawyer couldn't possibly want all of it for the work they've been doing, I mean, my God, how long have they been at it, only a few days." He looked at me and we remembered that Nichole had just denounced us both, walked out, and neither one of us had gone after her. We looked toward the door.

In the alcove behind *The Garden of Eden: Before and After*, a group broke out singing "For He's a Jolly Good Fellow." Others had gone out on the patio to pour champagne on the people in the street below and deliver the good news. I left Cosmo with Blaine, who was trying to console him, and wandered around the gallery, listening to people talk about the news. They speculated on the amount of fines Harper had to pay, bidding into the hundreds of thousands. They offered nominees among the Provincetown painters they thought would accompany Harper to the Temple in Malibu, to paint the Jaguar mural. Someone started a rumor that Harper was coming home incognito, by private yacht, to avoid the fuss of reporters and well-wishers, while others planned the homecoming reception. There was even talk of a parade down Commercial Street to the wharf—a reception reserved only for the Bishop for the Blessing of the Fleet, followed by a ceremonial baptism, which could be achieved, someone suggested, by throwing Harper into the bay. It appeared that the information about Harper receiving royalties from the Temple of the Jaguar exhibit proceeds was common knowledge, and some people imagined the enormous popularity of the exhibit. They said the lines for it would wind through the Getty Museum grounds like those for the Pirates of the Caribbean ride at Disneyland; they described the people on Sunset Boulevard, Santa Monica Beach, Fifth Avenue and Soho wearing Harper's string ties and fedoras during the day, then dressing up for the evening in Mayan Ballplayer's garb, and the Goddess of Sin's fish-head skirts and squid necklaces. Someone imagined rubber and plastic dolls of the skeleton man, the whistling couple and the two-headed woman, sold in the museum shop, with contraband copies sold downtown on the sidewalks of Venice, and in the boutiques in Chelsea.

After circulating throughout the gallery, I ended up at the bar, where the more restrained celebrants were drinking scotch and bourbon, discussing the possible ways the remains of the Defense Fund money would be spent and keeping their eye on the television for news about Harper. "So what's going on?" I asked Lance, and pointed to the television.

"They've brought in specialists. The economist says that Harper's release is a victory for free enterprise. The foreign affairs advisor says that, thanks to Harper, with the nation's heightened awareness of our military presence in

Nicaragua, we'll be less likely to repeat the catastrophe of Vietnam."

***

On Sunday afternoon, those people who were in-the-know sat on the cement retainer wall at St. Mary's of the Harbor beach, or stood in the church parking lot behind it, drinking beer and scanning the horizon for the yacht that would bring Harper Martin back to Provincetown. Lydia Street straddled the wall and drank a Heineken. The parrot Sydney Greenstreet was perched on Lydia's shoulder, pacing back and forth restlessly, as if he were impatient for Harper to arrive. He was carrying a miniature American flag in his beak, and if anyone took it out he would immediately squawk: "Welcome Home, Harper! Welcome Home, Harper!" until they put the flag back in again.

Getz leaned against his jeep in the St. Mary's parking lot, talking to Lance and Angelo about the new Ice House renovations they could see were taking shape next door, and the bad news they had heard on television, that one of Harper's figurines was reported missing from the crates the federal government had returned. Joe approached them and peered into the jeep, which had been stocked with cases of champagne that the welcomers planned to uncork as soon as the yacht came ashore. Joe showed them Harper's photograph on the cover of the *New York Times*, and told them about the missing figurine; they said they already knew.

I went for a walk on the beach below St. Mary's and stopped to inspect the Ice House renovations. They must have started building overnight, the minute they had received word that Harper had been released. Workers installed plumbing and wiring walls and windows went up, the existing brick and concrete were being repaired and augmented. Landscapers planted shrubs around the periphery of the building and installed window boxes; roofers measured for skylights and laid down tar paper; the parking lot was being leveled and scraped and poured with a layer of broken shells; there were even carpenters out on the old boat launch, replacing the rotted boards.

Whitney approached me and stood with me awhile, watching the renovations.

"I thought you rebuilt in stages," she said, "first the plumbing and wiring, then the walls and roof, then the parking lot, then the landscaping, then the boat launch, then the mailboxes, then maybe a few umbrellas and *chaises longues*."

"That would be the sane way to do it," I said and patted Whitney on the shoulder. I turned and walked up the beach toward St. Mary's.

"I guess we've all gone crazy then."

"It looks that way." I started to climb the buttress up to the retainer wall.

"I got an apprenticeship with Helen Frankenthaler in New York. She saw the *Incident in Fialta* on the Harper Martin Profile and wants me to work with her."

"That's great. So what are you so gloomy about?"

"Elaine's not coming to New York with me."

I sat on the wall and looked down at her. "She won't come?"

"She says I really like boys, that I'm just on a holiday from them."

"Is it true?"

Whitney shrugged. “How the hell would I know? I don’t know anything anymore. I mean, how did they get the Ice House fixed up so fast? Nobody was there yesterday. Have they been working all night?” Whitney wandered off down the beach, shaking her head.

Mary was leaning against the wall of the church itself, talking to Raphael Souza, who was more nervous than usual because he had been elected to give the speech on Harper’s behalf at the end of the parade, when they reached the wharf. Raphael spotted Whitney coming toward them from the beach and waved to her. She waved back, started to climb the concrete buttress over the retainer wall, then changed her mind, jumped back down into the sand, and stood there looking out to sea.

“Kate! Kate!” Angelo yelled. He ran up to me from behind and draped all his cameras over my neck and shoulders, one by one.

“I’m beginning to feel the weight of your predicament,” I said.

“Kate, Kate, guess what I got?” he said, and sat down next to me on the retainer wall.

“Your own pet Killer Whale.”

“A book contract with The Sierra Club. They want me to move to Greenland for the winter, live with the Eskimos there, and then write a book about Polar Bears.”

“You’ll freeze. When do you leave?”

“In a few days.” He tugged at one of his cameras. “Aren’t you excited for me?”

“Of course. Oh, and you can use the footage of me and the dolphin.”

“Fantastic. You’re such a sweetheart.” He lifted the cameras from me, kissed me on the cheek, and walked down the wall toward Lydia Street and Sydney Greenstreet, taking pictures of them along the way.

Mary left Raphael at the wall of the church and sat down next to me, her back to the bay. "Have your forgiven yourself yet?" she said.

"For which crime?" I asked

"For everything."

I spotted a boat on the horizon and whispered: "Is that him?"

Mary twisted around to look. She shook her head. "Just a trawler."

"So what about you?" I tried to ask after Mary's news, since it was not as forthcoming as other people's.

"I've decided to go to Boston this winter and live with my dad. Keep him company. This first winter is going to be rough."

"Your dad likes me."

Mary laughed. "I guess you'll have to come visit."

"I guess." I shifted my position on the wall. "Will you bring Grace with you?"

Mary stood up in the parking lot, and walked behind me. "Why would I bring Grace?" she said, and began to massage my shoulders.

"I just thought it would be nice."

"Elaine wants to go. She feels bad now that she cut Whitney loose."

"Maybe Whitney will go down to New York, check out the scene, realize the grass isn't greener and insist Elaine comes down to visit her. Then they'll get back together."

"Maybe. I think that's what Elaine is hoping." She patted me on the back. "You can come visit you know."

"I know," I said. "I will." I turned around to see Mary, who gave me a kiss on the forehead.

"In the meantime, work on forgiving yourself," she said, knocked me lightly upside the head, and walked back to the church to talk to Raphael, who had been joined by Edward with his blind collie. They stood together pointing at the Ice House, admiring the renovations. Edward thought the umbrellas and *chaise longues* should be blue to match the cornflowers in the window boxes, but Raphael insisted they should be green or yellow.

Getz sat down next to me. "The Voodoo Woman says I have a magnet inside me," I explained. "You know what she says about you? She says you're indelible."

"That's what all the girls say about me," he said, and then laughed quietly to himself.

I did not think I had ever seen him laugh, and told him so. He bowed his head and kicked the retainer wall with the heels of his sandals. "It's true. Usually I'm too serious. But with all this going on"—he waved his hand around at the beach and the parking lot—"you just have to laugh. I mean really, don't you think it's funny?" I agreed that it was. "Nothing's ever got to me like this. It's really funny."

"Getz, can I ask you something?" He put his hands down on the wall and nodded. "Why did you drop me over the whale watch boat?"

"Gabe asked me to. He said it would help you. I trusted him, and I knew you were safe."

"And it didn't matter that I hadn't agreed to it, that I didn't know what was going on?"

Getz looked at me with that severe, intense look he usually wore. "You call most of the shots," he said. "I didn't think one moment against your will would hurt. And if I'd thought he had something mean in mind, I would have talked him out of it."

He held my glance. I thought he could have looked at me forever and not broken his glance. Nothing unsettled him. I wondered if this were the way he was at night; if this were part of his charm. And suddenly it occurred to me that, if he was so wise, maybe he knew—maybe he knew about my amnesia—and just didn't feel the need to say anything about it. That would be just like Getz.

"Are you going to come with us when we go paint the mural?" He squinted into the sun to check the water for incoming yachts.

"Who's we?" I said.

"Harper will want me and Joe and Gabe to help. I don't know who else."

"Maybe I'll visit."

After Getz left Joe jumped up on the wall and began to shout: "That's the one! That's the one!"—and pointed somewhere out past the breakwater. Getz ran to the back of the jeep, and distributed the champagne bottles. Lydia Street unrolled a large sign that said: WELCOME HOME HARPER MARTIN, PROVINCETOWN'S HERO attached at both ends to wooden posts, and planted them in the sand facing the water. Lance shouted: "You'd think this was the remake of *From Here To Eternity.*" In all the commotion Sydney Greenstreet's miniature flag was knocked out of his beak and he began to squawk: "WELCOME HOME HARPER! WELCOME HOME HARPER!" until Lance muttered: "What a pain in the clitoris," and shoved it back in again.

The boat was clearly in sight now, and lots of people

stood up on the retainer wall to look, waving the champagne bottles, shouting, cheering, blowing whistles and horns. The Voodoo Woman opened two boxes filled with felt fedoras and leather string ties just like Harper's, and passed them out to everyone who was willing to wear them. She explained she received all sorts of mail order clothes catalogues working at Grace's djellaba store, even for military apparel and safari gear, so when she saw these she had ordered a few cases of them on the sly.

Dominic appeared on his windsurfer with Blaine riding on the back; they did a few spins around the St. Mary's Beachfront and Ice House boat launch before heading out to meet the yacht. When Angelo saw them he howled, jumped down from the retainer wall, losing his fedora, and ran along the water line, taking pictures of them with each of the three cameras he had strapped over his shoulders.

When Harper was in sight, standing on the front deck of the boat, waving, a television van screeched into the St. Mary's parking lot, and the camera crew jumped out, running to the retainer wall with their cameras already rolling, like bandits with their guns cocked, come to rob a moving train. "Who told these pencil-necked geeks we were going to be here?" Lance yelled.

When he reached land, Harper tipped his hat and bowed. He pointed to the people who were wearing hats like his, and read his welcome home sign. Lydia brought Sydney Greenstreet to him. When Harper took the miniature flag out of his mouth, Sydney squawked: "ORANGE JUICE PLEASE!" and, "UNITED STATES OUT OF NICARAGUA!: until Lydia reminded him what he had just learned, and he greeted Harper properly.

Harper shook Joe's hand and thanked him for the flowers Joe had sent to him in jail. "Look," Harper said. "I want to call a meeting at eight tonight. Can you get some people together?" Joe said he would, and Harper explained that he wanted to introduce some painters to the work involved in recreating the Temple of the Jaguars mural, the time it would take, the salaries and personal publicity they could expect, and see who was willing to help.

"Tell me who to invite," Joe said, wrote the names on the cover of the *New York Times*, and showed Harper his photograph.

While Joe was writing down the names, Angelo cut in and thanked Harper for the book contract on the Polar Bears in Greenland. "The CBS documentary and all the other stuff, it never would have happened without your Temple of the Jaguars Story."

Harper tried to tell him to forget it. "Hey, your career marches on to its inexorable conclusion no matter what I do or don't do." But Angelo, with his three cameras, just kept snapping photographs of Harper, and thanking him for everything.

"Whatever happens, it's all your fault," Angelo said. "You've launched my career." The Mother of the Year did likewise (except without the cameras), thanking Harper for her modeling contract with the Casablancas Agency. Then Harper noticed Raphael and Antaeus waving to him from the St. Mary's of the Harbor parking lot. Harper jumped the retainer wall in a dramatic gesture that made the crowd shriek and thrilled the TV cameramen, and hurried across the parking lot to shake hands with the investors of Maniac Drifter Inc. By this time the parade cars were lining up on

Commercial Street in preparation to drive Harper through town to the Wharf. Some of them spotted Harper, so all the cars on the street began to honk. The three men decided it was time to join the parade.

Raphael told Harper: "Your Corvette is parked over at Don's Café. Run down there and bring it this far, and I'll drive you through the parade. You can sit on the back and wave."

Harper looked around and noticed me sitting on the bumper of the jeep, drinking champagne from a plastic glass. "Ride with me. Raphael offered to drive the Corvette."

"I don't remember what we talked about, Harper," I said, hurrying over with him to Commercial Street, and waving to everyone in the front of the parade line as they whizzed east toward the end of the line, where Harper's Corvette was parked at Don's Café. "If I was supposed to do something for you, I haven't done it."

"There wasn't anything to do," he said, and squeezed my elbow so I would run faster. He took the plastic cup and threw the champagne back in one swig like it was a shot of whiskey. "Don't worry about it now. We'll talk later."

Harper's homecoming parade was as spectacular as the ones for Blessing of the Fleet and Fourth of July, if not quite as stunning or outrageous as the costume parade the transvestites staged at the end of the season. At the head of the procession, Falzano drove a red Chevrolet Impala with white interior; Paradiso's singers Paula and Christianne stood in the back, Christianne in her white tuxedo and Paula in a black evening gown. They sang "New York New York," "When You Get Lost Between the Moon and New York City," and all the Frank Sinatra songs they could think of.

The fire engines from Pumpers Number Four and Five carried the soccer and little league teams through the parade, waving miniature American flags and blowing horns. Joshua recruited the skateboarders to catch rides alongside the convertibles and fire engines; hanging on to their bumpers with one hand, and waving to the crowd with the other. Slashette had commissioned a flatbed truck to carry her and her Fashion Espionage escort-spies; they lurked on the flatbed in their black trench coats and sunglasses, their hands in their pockets, eyeing the crowd suspiciously, hiding behind each other and occasionally pulling their squirt guns to spray people. Getz drove the Mother of the Year and the Voodoo Woman in the jeep; the Mother had changed into her Goddess of Sin costume and the Voodoo Woman into her scarf and drapery outfit; they sat in the back of the jeep, tossing the remaining fedoras and string ties to the crowd. Antaeus drove a convertible Thunderbird he had rented up-Cape especially for the occasion; Cosmo and Lydia Street rode in the front with Sydney fluttering between them and screaming: "HARPER MARTIN! HARPER MARTIN!"

Lance and Angelo rode on top of the Rescue Squad ambulance, Lance shouted: "Sit on A Happy Face!" to the crowd, and Angelo took pictures of their reactions.

When we finally reached the end of the wharf, a crowd had assembled there, some on the dock itself and others in the boats. Someone threw a squid into Harper's Corvette, the way an adoring fan might throw flowers onto the stage at a rock concert. Then another fan tossed a lobster into the car, then a cod flew in, then some of the fedoras and string ties that the Voodoo Woman had distributed sailed into the car, then some champagne corks and plastic glasses followed, until whatever spare accessory people had with them were thrown to Harper: fish tackle, bobbins, rubber boots, plastic buckets, clams and scallops, suspenders, old socks, jar lids—whatever was at hand.

Falzano drove Christianne and Paula up to the front of the line, where they sang "The Man I Love" to Harper, and then, "I Get A Kick Out of You." Afterward they gave the microphone to Harper. "All that time in the slammer, I thought about you guys," he told them. The crowd howled. Harper thanked them for their support. "I wouldn't have come home from that joint so soon if it hadn't been for your help during Benefit Week." The crowd cheered and threw more debris at him. He told them that the investors of Maniac Drifter Inc. had decided to donate the remaining money from the Harper Martin Defense Fund to AIDS research, and to restore the Historical Plaque houses in Provincetown. Everyone applauded.

Raphael took the microphone away from him. "Don't you think Harper Martin is too modest," he said. The crowd screamed.

"Oh, don't be a dope," Harper said.

"Not only has he brought commerce and success to himself and Provincetown," Raphael went on, but the crowd was yelling so much it was difficult to hear him. Joe and Getz climbed up on the Corvette, lifted Harper out by his arms, and carried him over to the edge of the wharf. As they held him by his hands and feet and swung him over the water, the crowd yelled the countdown, and on three, Getz and Joe threw him out into the water. On his way down he lifted his hat to the crowd. They jumped in the water after him.

Raphael was trying to describe Harper as a household word, as a star, as a hero not only for Provincetown but for the nation, not just because he circumvented specious trade regulations to bring the Temple artifacts into the country, but because he cured the nation's amnesia about its own history, to be precise, about Vietnam, and made Americans aware of their country's role in Nicaragua.

But no one was listening to Raphael. Most everyone had jumped into the bay, and was swimming, splashing, talking, climbing into the boats and diving out again. Even the Orca surfaced near Harper and disappeared again. But Lance walked over to Raphael, who was still holding the microphone in his hand, and said to him, "This could only happen now, when a Hollywood movie actor is serving his second term as president."

Someone took the miniature American flag out of Sydney Greenstreet's beak, and he shouted: "SIT ON A HAPPY FACE!" He perched on Lance's shoulder, and rode on it, while Lance climbed into the Corvette and rummaged through the debris that had accumulated on the jump seat.

***

I took advantage of the confusion to search for Nichole. I could not find her at the wharf, or on Commercial Street, so I went back to her house. I knocked and knocked on her door but no one answered. I could not hear any hammering or sawing, or the persistent disco beat of the Jane Fonda Aerobics workout tape. The house was quiet, and that frightened me. I let myself in, walked through the kitchen, and stood in the middle of the living room, listening.

I knew Nichole might be gone; I would have been naive if the thought had not crossed my mind. But I never had any idea I would find the house completely empty. I was not prepared for that.

Everything was gone: the furniture, the rugs, the china from the cabinets, the looms and weavings, the canvases, even the gas and plumbing bills. And the rooms had been washed spotlessly clean, so there was not even a trace of dust, or lint, or crumbs, or wadded paper. In short, there was nothing to remember Nichole by, not even the most miniscule scrap. She had even denied us our grief. She was not willing to imagine us combing the rooms for souvenirs and memories. She had done it on purpose.

I lay down on the spotless wooden floor, which looked buffed like an old shoe. I stretched out with my feet facing north and my head under the south windows so I could hear the foghorns and see the sky. When I lay my head down I heard a loud click, and then the sound of static, as if a dull needle had been set down on the grooves of a scratched record. Then I heard Nichole's voice.

"Give it up, Kate," the voice said. "You won't see me again. You won't know where I am. So just give it up. When you see my father, you can tell him the same."

"She always did have a flair for the melodramatic," Cosmo said. He opened one of the built-in cabinets in the dining room, and pulled out the cassette player Nichole used to play her Jane Fonda Aerobics workout tape.

I sat up. "I didn't hear you come in," I said.

"She must have rigged up some kind of triggering device over there by the window. She probably figured that, when you were sufficiently shocked, stunned, and consumed by grief, you would walk over to the window and look out, a kind of lonely, nostalgic way to console yourself. And that was the moment she wanted to turn the knife." He put the cassette player back in the cabinet. "It's a part of her I've never seen before."

"What's on the flipside?" I went over to the cabinet, took the tape player from him, popped out the cassette and turned it over. "It says: *Buddy Holly's Greatest Hits*." I inserted the tape and pushed the play button.

Cosmo went into the kitchen, opened the cupboards and refrigerator, and looked inside, leaving the doors ajar, then, he sat down on the sink counter. The tape began to play "I'm So Devoted to You."

"So did it work?" he said. "Do you feel sufficiently wretched? Guilty? Sorry? Or do you just get mad? I mean what do you do at a time like this?" He looked out the kitchen window.

"Where's Frank?"

"At home. He decided to stay with his wife."

I wandered into Nichole's bedroom and looked out the window at the new porch. Cosmo followed me in. "I don't know what it's like," he began. "I mean I never had anyone close to me die. The worst thing that ever happened to me is when Charlotte decided to move away." Charlotte was the one Cosmo had had an affair with. "I heard your mother died when you were quite young. So correct me if I'm wrong, but somehow this seems like it would be worse. It seems so willful, so unnecessary."

"A lot of things are unnecessary," I said. I wandered back into the living room. He followed me. The tape played, "Whenever I want you all I have to do is dream."

"So should we go after her? Should we find her? Is that what she wants? What should we do?" I lay down on the floor again. Cosmo shrugged. "You don't give much away, do you?" he said. "Why don't you tell me what you think of all this?"

"Can I keep this tape?" I said. "And the player?" I sat up and started to cry.

"Please tell me." He sat down next to me.

"I can't," I said. "It's not my right."

"The hell with rights." He put his hand on my shoulder. "I'm asking you. I want to know."

"It won't help. I just keep thinking that the difference between you and Nichole is that when *you* had an affair, *you* didn't have to leave town."

"Nichole didn't have to leave town. Neither did Charlotte."

I stood up and waved my arms around at the empty, polished room. "You think this is just amateur theatrics?" I screamed. "How bad would she have to feel to be compelled to do this? How bad would she have to feel?"

"You don't know. She was born here. She grew up in this town. It's not just the way I reacted to her and Frank. It's not just your friend Whitney going over to the other side. It's a whole host of things, from the day she was born. It's like a bad marriage, 26 years of hurts and wounds that have never been healed. You haven't lived here. You don't know."

"I don't know! I don't know!" I screamed. "Of course, I don't know! So why the hell does everyone keep asking me things, like I was the Oracle of Delphi or something? You're right. I don't know. I don't know anything." I grabbed the cassette player out of the built-in cabinet and ran through the kitchen out the door. The machine had been playing "If you knew/ Peggy Sue/ Oh how my heart yearns for you," but when I ran I pulled the plug out of the socket, and the machine had stopped. It was quiet now. I slowed to a walk, held the cassette player to my ear and listened, as if I could hear whispering.

***

Monday

When I woke up Monday morning I was at home, in bed with Harper Martin, who was sitting up with a notebook on his knees, watching the CBS morning news.

"Hi, doll," he said when he saw my eyes were open. He kissed the top of my head. "How was your beauty rest?" He continued writing in his notebook.

"What are you doing?"

"I'm looking at the list of painters who are going to the Getty Museum with me, to help paint the Temple of the Jaguars Mural. Everyone said they'd come except Nichole and Cosmo."

"Why not Nichole and Cosmo?" I propped my head up on the pillows so I could see Dan Rather on the television set.

"No one can find Nichole, and Cosmo says he has to stay here and put her house up for sale."

"Can he do that? It's Nichole's house."

Harper shrugged. "Either way, he won't come." I was going to insist that Cosmo could not possibly sell a house that did not belong to him, and if Harper wanted, I would try to talk to Cosmo about going to Malibu to help paint the Jaguar Mural, but Harper put his hand on my arm to silence me and listened to Dan Rather on the *CBS Morning News*. Dan was saying that Harper's art dealer had thoroughly studied the returned crates and had reported the missing figurine as the lava stone figurine of the fertility god Xipe Totec. An inset photo of the skin-suit man flashed on the screen above Dan Rather's head. He reminded the viewers that the agreement with the Nicaraguan government stipulated all temple artifacts must be displayed together, so the Temple of the Jaguars exhibit at the Getty museum could not be opened to the public until the missing figurine was recovered.

Harper put the notebook down and sighed. "I guess we'll have to make a facsimile or something if the Feds can't find it."

"It'll turn up. Don't worry about it."

Harper looked at me. "I'm not worried. Listen, babe. You don't remember what we talked about?" I shook my head. "Well, I think we better discuss it now. I have to catch the plane back to Los Angeles in a few hours."

I sat up in bed. "Are you sure I didn't fail to do something you asked me to do? You can tell me if I did."

"That's not it. You spilled the beans. You told me about your amnesia."

"I did?" I cocked my head and looked at him quizzically.

"And you told me how your mother died."

"She died of lung cancer, didn't she?"

"You were there at her bed when she died. You told me what happened. Do you remember?"

I shook my head. "I didn't go see her the day she died."

Harper poured himself a glass of Jack Daniels, neat, from the bottle that was on the nightstand. He took a Marlboro out of the pack, ripped the filter off, put it in his mouth, and lit it. He took a long draw on the cigarette, blew the smoke away from me, and then took a sip of Jack Daniels. He stared at the television for a minute. While I watched him I thought to myself, *This isn't real. I'm in a movie. I'm in a goddamn movie.*

"You were sitting at her bedside. She reached out for your hand and you gave it to her. She was rigged up to one of those breathing machines. You said they make an eerie whirring noise. Anyway, she asked the doctor to take it off her face for a moment so she could ask you a question."

I pulled the covers up, looked at Harper as if to say, *Why are you doing this to me,* then burrowed into him, resting my face on his shoulder and wrapping my arms around him.

"Hold me," I said.

He put the Jack Daniels down and held me.

"Do you remember what she asked you?" He took another drag on the Marlboro and flicked the ashes into the ashtray on the nightstand.

"No," I said. "I don't. I don't remember."

Harper rested the cigarette in the ashtray, blew the smoke away, and then tried to lift my head up with his hand so he could look at me, but I kept it against his chest, and would not move. "Look me in the eye," he said.

"I can't."

"Your mother asked you to forgive her for something. Do you remember what it was?" He took another sip of bourbon.

"Did she ask me to forgive her for dying?"

"No, don't guess. Try to remember."

"I don't remember."

"You can't remember?"

"I can't remember," I repeated.

Harper emptied his glass of Jack Daniels, then lifted the bottle and poured himself another. From my position with my head lying against his chest, I watched his hands move, and tried to imagine the expression on his face—stubborn maybe, or grave, or just resigned. I felt him swallow the whiskey. I could hear his heart beating underneath his ribs. I lay my face down against his chest, where it was warm, and thought how nice it was to be this close to another human being. Not being able to remember intimacy, skin against skin, was like not having the intimacy, as if I had been deprived of human contact, of all touch, of all love.

"Do you remember now, what she asked you to forgive her for?"

I felt how warm his skin was against my face, listened to his heartbeat, and said, "No."

He put his whiskey and cigarette down, and gripped my arms with his hands. He tried to lift my head again, but I resisted. "You have to look at me, babe," he said.

"No," I said, and shook my head so it rubbed against his chest.

"She asked you," he said, and stopped to take another swig of whiskey. I put my hand on his arm and gripped it as hard as I could. It's not real, I kept telling myself. It's not really happening. It's a movie.

"She asked me if I would forgive her—" I said, finally.

He sighed and my head rode up and down on his chest, like swimming with the dolphin.

"She asked me to forgive her for not loving me." There. I had said it.

He tried to look at me again but I still would not let him. He poured himself another drink, and then held on to me with both hands, while I started to shake, and then buck and convulse, like someone going through withdrawals, and then finally started to cry.

"I'm sorry, babe," he said. "I'm sorry."

He held me and rubbed my head, and pushed my hair out of my face, and wiped the tears off my chin with the back of his hand. Finally, when I had been crying quite a long time, I let him lift my face up, and look at it.

***

Tuesday, Malibu California

The entire Temple of the Jaguars exhibit was closed to the public until the mural could be completed and the Xipe Totec figurine recovered, but Harper had left my name with the Getty Museum officials, so one of the guards had provided me with a map, walked me to the gate of the Mayan metropolis, unlocked it, and let me inside.

The Temple of the Jaguars facsimile had been constructed on a hill overlooking the ocean. But instead of simply building the one temple that was required, and displaying an artist's rendering of the other buildings to show what the Mayan metropolis would have looked like, the

Getty Museum had reconstructed the entire cluster of buildings, including the House of Governors, the Nunnery, the Pyramid of the Magician, the High Priest's Grave, the Hieroglyphic Stairway leading to the Temple of the Jaguars, the Skull Rack Platform, the Steam Bath and Ball Court, and even the Well of Sacrifice.

The Getty designers intended that the Temple of the Jaguars should be the most elaborate and spectacular of the buildings in the Mayan metropolis. The Hieroglyphic Stairway that led up the pyramid platform to the temple had been decorated with relief carvings of costumed men with feathered headdresses and trapezoidal wings emerging from their hips who carried long-handled fans. The pyramid platform supporting the Temple of the Jaguars had been built so high that it provided a vista from which you could see the entire metropolis. The entrance to the Temple of the Jaguars faced west, and from the doorway, visitors could see the sunset over the Pacific.

The serpent mask doorframe, with its teeth lining the sill, fangs protruding from the jambs, and serpent's nose and eyes above, had been installed around the entrance to the Temple of the Jaguars, so that, when you walked inside the temple, you were actually walking into the serpent's mouth. In the outer chamber of the temple, the Getty curators had displayed some of the figurines from the confiscated crate: the skeleton man, the two faced woman, the whistling couple. They had left one glass case empty for Xipe Totec—the skin-suit man.

Inside the inner chamber of the Temple of the Jaguars, Harper and our painter friends worked on the mural. Canvas had been laid down on the floor of the room, and a huge table stood in the middle of it, cluttered with plans and drawings. Along the walls the battle and ritual scenes had been sketched in, and each painter had been assigned one to fill in with colors.

Joe worked on the south wall, painting a picture of siege operations during a battle. Warriors in profile wearing feathered headdresses brandished round shields against a frenzy of flying lances. Getz painted the east wall, which depicted a ruler performing penance with his family. Cedric was at work on the north wall, painting in a landscape of a seacoast village. At the front of this mural the sea was represented by a stack of wavy lines, and in it were warriors in canoes, paddling to the left, while crabs, octopus and fish lurked in the squiggly lines underneath their boats. On shore, women with receding hairlines ground corn, carried baskets on their backs and walked with sticks, or sat complacently in the huts watching snakes dance. Huge birds shaped like geese flew toward the ground, as if they would crash. Between the huts were thick trees with forked branches and a ball of leaves on each side.

Harper painted the west wall, which showed a human sacrifice by heart excision. Above the door, Gabe sketched in a god impersonator, lying on his back across the lintel, with serpents rising from his belt.

When they finally noticed me, I was standing in the entryway to the inner chamber with an empty pillowcase slung over my shoulder, listening to Joe tell the rest of them about the new gay bar Raphael Souza planned to open with the profits from his investment in Maniac Drifter Inc. "Hi guys," I said.

"Asheva, asheva, asheva," Cedric said in greeting, and jutted his elbows at me. Then he began to grind his teeth together.

"Hey, babe," Joe said. "I knew you'd come. I knew you couldn't live without us. You're addicted."

"It's Kate," Gabe said, as if he had not known I was coming.

Getz brushed his hair out of his eyes and smiled at me. "Yo, Kate," he said.

I began to wander around and look at the different scenes in the mural. "I can't believe this place," I said. "I thought they were just going to build the one temple."

"Isn't it outrageous?" Joe said.

"So why'd they do it?" I said.

"They have two million a month to spend in acquisition money," Cedric explained. "And the Temple of the Jaguars exhibit seemed so promising, it was getting such good press and attracting so many visitors to the museum before the exhibit had even opened, that they figured, why build just one temple? Why not thrill the public and build the whole Mayan city?"

"Isn't it amazing?" Harper said.

"It's incredible," I said. "It's enormous. First, I thought they were just fake fronts, like a stage set at the movie studios, or you couldn't walk on them, or there wasn't anything inside, but they're real buildings. It's outrageous. It's like Disneyland."

"Disneyland for the art set," Cedric said. "I used to think Provincetown was like Disneyland gone haywire. But now it's been outdone."

"I think it's wonderful," Gabe said quietly. "I really do."

Harper pulled me aside where no one else could hear us. He slipped the pillowcase off my shoulder, unfurled it, looked at both sides, waving it like a matador taunting a bull, and then returned it to my shoulder. He whispered: "Can you remember everything?" I shook my head. "Can you remember what we discussed?"

"Of course. I told you that my mother asked me to forgive her for before she died."

"What did she ask you to forgive her for?"

"For not loving me."

"And you can't remember everything? You can't remember what happens at night?"

"No," I said.

Harper put his arm around me. "What a dope," he said, roughing up my hair. "What a pal. What a sucker." He gripped my shoulders. "Maybe you'll remember from now on. What do you think?" I shrugged underneath the weight of his hands.

I looked at Cedric and his seacoast village, Getz and his ruler performing penance, Joe and his siege operations, Gabe and his god impersonator, Harper and his heart excision—which one of them loved me? I did not know, I could not remember. That was the bliss and the glory of it. I did not know if they loved me. I did not know if I wanted them to love me. I did not know if they had failed to love me.

I could not remember these men. Did I love one of them? How could I? After all, weren't the memories of past intimacies what love was? If I could not remember I could not love. And I could not know who loved me back.

Cedric did not want me—he had left me a year before. That was easy enough. Gabe did not want me—he had told me I would hurt his feelings too much and it was too late. Getz and Joe did not want me. They had never indicated as much; they had never asked me for any exclusivity or commitment. So that left Harper.

I looked at Harper. "The babe's in love with me," he said. "You know what I mean?" He hugged me.

"We'll be at Harry's Bar," Joe said.

Gabe let out one of his world-weary sighs.

"You can always change your mind!" Joe yelled as they were going out the door, and waved goodbye with his gloved hand.

"Asheva Asheva!" Cedric called.

When they were gone, Harper said, "What are you thinking about?"

I had been thinking that my amnesia was like dreams or intuition, I knew something, but I did not know how. Harper took my hand and led me into the outer chamber where the figurines were displayed. He went over to the glass case reserved for the skin-suit man, opened it, and took him out.

"I was thinking that failing to love someone is not a crime."

Harper turned the skin-suit man around in his hands. With his finger he stroked his chest where the stitches were. He poked his finger into the mouth of the mask, and felt for the mouth underneath. "Then what's the crime?"

"The crime is not forgiving."

Harper handed me the skin-suit man. "I was the one who took him," I said. "Well, you must know now. I always intended to bring him back."

"You know when I fell in love with you?" He took the

skin suit back and held him in his hands. "At the White Sands Costume Ball, when I saw you in my clothes. It's not narcissism. You'd found a way inside me, and occupied this same space with me. The same way this little guy does." He handed the skin-suit man back to me.

"Letting the god inside you."

"What do you think of him?"

"I think he's revolting. And I think he's sublime." I put him back into the glass case.

I longed for the intimacy of whispering and touching, the accumulated repertoire of gestures and signs.

We stepped through the serpent's mouth to the outside, and watched the red sun sink down into the ocean. "Love is like that sometimes," he said, pointing at it.

"I wouldn't know," I said, and leaned the full weight of my body against him.

Acknowledgements

This novel was written with the assistance of a National Endowment for the Arts Grant, a Wallace E. Stegner Fellowship at Stanford University, a Grace Foundation Fellowship at the Fine Arts Work Center Provincetown, and artist residencies at Yaddo, Millay and Montalvo Center for the Arts. Special thanks to Paul Nelson and Michael Mirolla.

About The Author

Laura Marello is the author of *Claiming Kin, The Tenants of the Hotel Biron, Balzac's Robe, The Gender of Inanimate Objects and Other Stories*, and several other books. She is the recipient of a National Endowment for the Arts Grant, a Wallace E. Stegner Fellowship from Stanford University, a Fine Arts Work Center fellowship, a Vogelstein Grant and a Deming grant. She has enjoyed writer's residencies at Yaddo, MacDowell Colony, Millay Colony, Montalvo Center for the Arts, and the Djerassi Foundation.

Printed in January 2017
by Gauvin Press,
Gatineau, Québec